ABOUT THE AUTHOR

Claire Merchant is an Australian author and storyteller. She is best known for her collection of fantasy, contemporary, and romance novels set in fictional South Coast. In 2018, Claire was voted one of the '50 Great Writers You Should Be Reading' by The Authors Show.

MIDNIGHT MISTRY

...Such is Death

ALSO BY CLAIRE MERCHANT

Mistry by Moonlight

South Coast Son

Foresight

Forever Ruby

Knowing Nora

Mistry at Dawn

A Lady Born, A Pirate Bred

Christian and Layla

Finding Hope

Dreaming of Reality

Linger

Heart Strings

Daughter Departed

Ebony Rose

Light and Shadow: The Story of Luna Lake

For everyone who has found strength in their weakness

Acknowledgements

I am very blessed to be surrounded by my own little mystical support network. Thank you to my friends and family who accept my need to spend time in South Coast, and never seem to be surprised when I talk about various conversations that I've had with a grim reaper.

Thank you to everyone who has supported me, and who continues to support me, both domestically and across the globe. It means the world to me.

To everyone who has read my books, given me feedback, laughed with me, cried with me, and just generally felt excited about turning the page – thank you, sincerely. Writing is my passion, and hearing that you can relate to my characters and stories is very special. Thank you for being you.

Be yourself. Be brave. Be kind.
Claire x

Preface

The End of the Beginning

It wasn't supposed to be like this. The hard part was supposed to be over. I was only twenty-two, and I'd already escaped from the grips of death twice, once from natural causes, once from the supernatural. On both occasions, the man of my life had been my saviour – my father when I was a child, and then when I grew up, my boyfriend. But now? Now *I* was the danger to those that I loved.

I faced the side effect of living.

Nothing came without a consequence.

You can't escape death.

You can't *kill* death without it changing you – and *boy*, did it change me.

I thought that I had gone through enough alterations in the last year and a half to last a lifetime, but it turns out that it was nothing compared to what was coming, what change was happening, had happened, without anyone realising.

Now what?

What do I do?

What does anyone do when they realise that they have no

control over themselves, or over any of the changes that are happening, and have happened?

I had my friends, my cavalry, which I never could have survived without. They were my supernatural support that fought for my life when I had been marked with death. They had protected me, hunted for me, and killed for me when all they knew about me was that I had unknowingly laid down my own life for one of them – one of the collectively mythological beings that resided in South Coast, who manage to stay mostly undetected by humans.

I was the only exception.

Until now.

Such is death.

Phase One

The Full Moon

"Seriously, Ruby," I sighed. "Thanks for having me over. I always hate this time of the month."

"Please, Taylor," the stunning blonde vampire replied, rolling her silver eyes. "You know that you're always welcome. Besides, Cole and Harper are off having a boy's night, it seems only fitting that we have a girl's night."

I smiled. "Have you heard anything from Hunter since... everything?"

It had been a little over a week since Harper had returned to South Coast, or rather, returned to me. In the seven weeks that he was away, it never occurred to me that my makeshift protection detail would stay in touch, or in Hunter's case, disappear altogether.

"No." Ruby frowned. "Not a word."

I couldn't help but feel responsible for the beautiful, yet cynical, were-panthers disappearance. After all, the last time I had seen her, she had been wounded defending my life. It didn't surprise me that she didn't want to be around me, especially when she had been so fervent that Harper would

13

leave and never return. She had been so convinced that he was, and always would be, a lone wolf. Yet, that all seemed to change the night that I had saved his life on the side of the road, or had it been before then? Maybe it was when he had first spotted me in Italy. I shuddered at the memory because it was then that I had also met Leo, a wolf-hunter, who not only deceived me but forced death to follow me around. If it weren't for his presence in my life, none of the danger would have been brought into Harper's either. But then maybe I never would have discovered the whole supernatural underworld of South Coast.

"Are you all right, Taylor?" Ruby asked, eyeing me with concern. "He'll be okay, you know, Cole won't let him be seen or harmed in wolf form."

"I know." I nodded. The night before Full Moon, the Waxing Gibbous night, was one my least favourite nights on the lunar calendar. The worst was the Full Moon, since Harper's wolf side was at its apex then, meaning he had the least control over his form and behaviour. Then there was the night after the Full Moon when the Waning Gibbous was at its peak. He still turned into a wolf then, but it wasn't as painful, and it wasn't for as long. Those three nights without him reoccurred every month – every Moon cycle.

I hated thinking of it because I knew how it made him. I knew that he'd lose control of himself and physically burst out of his skin. I also knew that it worried him to be away from me. I was just glad he wasn't alone.

"It's our first night apart since he came back," I murmured.

14

"Three days feel like a mini-eternity."

"It's only thirty-six hours," she answered. "It's not forever."

I frowned into my glass of water.

"Sorry I'm late," said a voice after a puff of maroon smoke. "Traffic was a nightmare."

Ruby smiled at the new addition, the Shadow Weaver, who, again, gave my ego a bruising. She was quite short, with long hair the colour of fire that fell down to her tiny waist. Unlike the vampire across from me, she had copper skin, which was several shades lighter than her dark brown eyes.

"Taylor, this is Eden Marrone, Ebony and Rob's daughter," Ruby said. "Eden, this is Harper's girlfriend, Taylor Mistry."

"The human who was marked, right?" She smiled ruefully. "It's a pleasure."

I blinked at the girl who looked about the same age as me. "How can you be Ebony's daughter? Ebony doesn't look old enough to have an adult daughter."

"Shadow Weavers don't show aging after they hit adulthood." She shrugged.

"Ebony is actually a year older than my mother," Ruby said. "They used to work together at the *South Coast Courier*."

My mind was a boggle. "But then how old are you?"

"Twenty-something." She shrugged. "I don't keep count any more. I'm a few years older than Ruby, not that you can tell since I guess we both stopped aging at around twenty-one."

I shook my head. "Okay, so, forgive me, but *what* is a Shadow Weaver? Cole said something about you being like

15

witches?"

"Shadow magic," Ruby replied. "But, Eden isn't just any Weaver, she's a very powerful full-blood Weaver *born* under a red Moon."

I bit my lip. I had no idea what that actually meant or how it made a difference. "Oh."

"Shadow Weavers aren't usually born, they more possess a gene mutation in the blood and come into their powers when they get older, under a red Moon," Eden explained. "But since I have two Weaver parents, and was born under the red Moon, it triggered the change, and magic, at birth."

"Oh." I nodded.

Ruby breathed a laugh. "Taylor is still new to this supernatural world. She kind of fell head-first into the deep end."

"I'll say," I murmured. "Does silver hurt you too?"

Eden blinked. "No."

"I don't mean to offend you, but it seems to be a common aversion amongst the mystical, um, beings."

Eden laughed. "Well, Weavers are human where it counts—"

"Like Wendigos," Ruby added.

Eden made a face. "Except that *we* don't eat people, and we don't age because of the healing qualities we have in our blood. Other than that, we're just humans with magic powers."

"Oh, right." I shrugged. "Sure."

"Like Light Lacers," Ruby said, taking a sip from a black cup.

16

Eden's features darkened. "Mm, well."

"Light Lacers?" I asked. "I think I remember Rob mentioning them. What are they?"

Eden rolled her eyes. "The enemy."

"Your enemy, not ours," Ruby answered. "They're the white, well, light magic breed. They're born with abilities and come into full power at twenty. Cole says that they're nature's balancers to the Weaver."

"Except for the fact that there aren't many of those left any more," Eden said.

"But didn't Rob say something about someone being part both?" I frowned. "How does that work if you're opposites?"

"How do you and Harper work?" Eden shrugged. "It's not any different, crossing kinds happen, but they're not common. We have a natural aversion to Lacers, and it didn't end well for Joel's parents. It never ends well when different breeds mix."

I frowned.

"But she doesn't mean you and Harper," Ruby said. "Do you, Eden?"

"No, sorry, no." She smiled. "I meant, well you two are compatible. He's still human, he—"

"Just turns into a wolf three nights a month," I sighed. Eden and Ruby laughed, and I shook my head. "Yeah."

"Well, let's not talk about things that we can't control," Ruby said, clapping her pale hands together. "Taylor, let me get you a refill. Eden, can I get you anything?"

"Got any top shelf?"

Ruby's eyebrow lifted over her silver eyes. "I take it you

don't mean royal blood?"

"Whatever you have is fine." Eden grinned as I passed my glass to Ruby. She flittered away, and Eden shuffled closer to me.

"So what's it like, you know, with a werewolf guy?" she asked. Her expression caused my nerves to pinch. I felt my entire face burn with embarrassment.

"What?" I breathed.

"Well, I haven't *met* Harper yet. I've been out of town since he's been in South Coast, but I've always wondered if like, the physical stuff would be the same with a werewolf guy or, like, a shape-shifter. Is it much different?"

I blinked. "You can't just ask me that."

"Why not? We're bonding, and I'm curious."

"That's really personal though."

Eden's lips broke into a smile. "You two haven't done it yet, have you?"

"That's none of your business."

"How long have you been together?"

I shook my head. "Only for like a week or so."

She sighed. "But you have, like, been with a guy before right? Or are you a unicorn?"

"A what?"

"A virgin." She smirked. "Which at twenty… what—?"

"I'm twenty-two."

Her lips pressed together. "Is as rare as a unicorn these days."

I tried to swallow, but my heartfelt lodged in my throat.

18

"I'm not discussing this with you."

"Are you religious? Is that why you haven't, you know."

"Eden, please." I huffed. "Stop."

"Or are you just waiting for the *'right guy',*" she asked. "Because if I were you, I would just jump Harper and get it over with. It's only going to get worse as your expectations grow. Sex generally isn't that great the first few times, so if you're expecting fireworks—"

"Eden, I said stop," I snapped. I wasn't a prude, well, I didn't think that I was, but I didn't feel comfortable talking about that sort of stuff with anyone. To me, intimacy between two people was something that wasn't meant to be discussed in public. It was something that should remain between two people. Okay, so maybe I was a prude.

"Fine," she sighed. "Man, I can't believe that you're a unicorn. I bet Harper isn't, he is an animal after all."

I stood up to leave the room as Ruby returned. "Taylor?"

"I just need, um, where is the bathroom?"

"Down the hall," she said, gesturing with her head since her hands were full. "Second door from the end on the left."

I nodded and pushed myself forward, hearing Ruby's reprimanding tone tell Eden that I'd been through a lot and to leave it alone. I should have known that she'd listened to our conversation. Vampire hearing was as good as werewolf hearing, or better, I didn't know for sure. I was only human, after all, nothing out of the ordinary.

It probably wasn't the smartest idea of mine to have a slumber party with a vampire and her Shadow Weaver friend

19

on a weeknight. Especially when I had a morning tutorial, and it was this close to the end of semester. The weeks since I had been back from Italy had seemed to drag on, but I probably wouldn't take them back. Except for the whole being marked with death, being hunted by supernatural creatures to fulfil that fate, and then having the love of my life disappear for seven weeks. But I suppose that life is about taking the bad with the good.

Ruby was kind enough to drop me into South Coast University the following morning, Full Moon day morning, after a protein-rich and balanced breakfast, which she had prepared for me. I never thought that I would click with the blonde vampire so much, but she really seemed to understand me and not judge my innate need to keep up a disciplined diet. It was hard enough losing twenty-two kilos in the first place, but now it was the harder part – the maintenance part. I had been back home in South Coast long enough to strike up some sort of a routine, but it wasn't really a healthy one until Harper got back. I wasn't proud of the way that I'd carried myself when he was away, resembling more of a zombie than a human while, but now that he was back, it felt like everything was right in the world.

I survived the Friday morning classes with several long black coffees. When I had finished my classes for the day, it was early afternoon, so I headed to the library to photocopy some *not for loan* books to study, and then called Ruby to come and pick me up.

Maybe I was a little more paranoid than the average person,

but after being stalked by a flesh-eating wendigo for four weeks, the reasonable side effect is acute suspicion to anyone showing any kind of curiosity for me. Especially from the boy with orange eyes that seemed to bore into me from across the library. His intense gaze made me uncomfortable so, after returning the book, I went to wait outside in the spitting rain for Ruby. I wasn't there long when I felt a shadow beside me. I turned to find the curious-looking boy running his hand through his pitch-black hair.

"Hey, my name is Sal," he said.

I frowned. "I'm Taylor."

"Taylor, okay."

I glanced to the side. "Okay?"

"Yup." He smiled. "Are you a philosophy major, Taylor?"

"No, I'm a science major, Sal."

"Science? Really?" His eyebrow lifted. "But some things have no explanation."

I shrugged. "Then they're not the things that are of interest to me."

"I find that *exceedingly* hard to believe," he said. "Tell me, Taylor, what's your surname?"

"Um, it's Mistry."

"Mistry?" He laughed. "Seriously?"

"Seriously."

He blinked. "No. Seriously? Your surname is Mistry? Like *mystery*-Mistry?"

I frowned. "Well, what kind of name is Sal?"

"It's Salvatore." He chuckled. "Salvatore Vincent. Actually,

Vincenzo, but since I'm not in Italy any more—"

I groaned and started to walk up the road. "Perfect, of course you're Italian."

"Do you have something against Italians?" he asked, walking after me.

"Not all Italians, just attractive ones that show me attention."

Sal laughed. "Wow, what? Is that what I'm doing? And you think I'm attractive?"

"I, ugh," I sighed, stepping off the curb to cross the road. "No, never mind."

"No, wait, Taylor," he called. "Listen, you don't know me, and I don't know you."

I rolled back on my heels and ran my hands through my hair. "Nice observation there, Sal. Maybe you should switch to a science major."

"What are you?" he asked suddenly. "Your vibe is just, not quite human."

My mouth fell open. "Excuse me?"

"You heard me. What are you?"

"Who even are you?"

"I'm Sal." He grinned. "Salvatore Vincent, remember?"

I folded my arms.

"Did you die?" he whispered, edging closer. "Because that might explain a little. It feels like your number has expired already."

"Seriously," I breathed. "Who the hell are you?"

From the corner of my eye, a black Jag pulled up beside me

22

with expert precision. Sal continued to stare at me as I stepped towards it, opened the door, and clambered in.

"Hey." Ruby smiled.

"Please drive," I whispered. Ruby hit the accelerator and pulled out into the one-way street. We reached the end of it in next to no time, and she made a quick turn, speeding away from the university grounds.

"What's up?"

I shook my head. "Nothing, just some guy that, well, it was really weird actually."

"How so?"

"He kept staring at me in the library, then followed me out. He seemed harmless, but then he asked me *what* I was, and said something about me not being human," I said. "He asked if I had died, and said something about my number being expired already."

Ruby pulled a face. "You smell human to me."

"Have you ever heard anything like that before? About numbers, or vibes, or something?"

"No, nothing."

"Do you think…? I mean, I did die when I was six and came back to life." I shrugged. "Or do you think… do you think that maybe he was referring to me being marked by the banshee?"

"But you're not marked any more," she answered. "You killed it."

I nodded.

"I wouldn't worry about him, Taylor, he seems a little

23

strange." She smiled. "Now do you have to work at the vet clinic today? Harper mentioned something about you still helping out there after uni on some days."

I shook my head. "Not today. Actually, not for a couple of weeks. My manager has given me some time off considering exams are only two weeks away. Next week is the last week of semester."

"I know, I'm studying through distance education," she answered.

"Cool, what are you studying?"

"Business."

I laughed. "Sounds, um, fun."

She laughed along. "It's interesting. I'm halfway through at the end of this semester. I figured that since I'm running *Crescent* now, it would be good to learn. I've already finished a law degree. I was a lawyer before I was turned into a vampire."

"Wow, really?" I sighed. "You didn't want to pursue it?"

"Well, I still have to be careful because, as far as everyone in my human life knows, I'm working in Spain," she said. "But I still help Cole out with his legal needs, considering he owns so many businesses. So it's not all bad."

"People think that you're in Spain?"

"Yes, it was my cover for disappearing."

"When… how long have you been a… a vampire for?"

She breathed a laugh. "It still sounds strange to me too. I've been this way for about five years."

"And Cole was the one who turned you. You said once that he saved you, right?"

24

"That's right, he did." She nodded.

"Have you been together all that time?"

Her head tipped, sending her blonde hair over her shoulder. "Mostly. It's been about four years that we've been... as we are now."

"Ridiculously in love?"

"Yes." She smirked. We both fell silent as she pulled into the drive that led underneath the garage of Cole's building.

"What about you and Harper?" she asked. "You two have been inseparable since he reappeared in your life, other than what the Moon cycle disallows."

I nodded. "I love him. I've never felt this way about anyone before. I feel like he's my other half, like, he's my fate."

"I know what you mean."

I blushed. "Sorry, I must sound really naïve considering Harper and I really have only been together for a little over a week."

"No, sometimes you just know." She shrugged. "Like love at first sight."

"Right, exactly."

"I'm thrilled that it worked out for the two of you." She nodded. "You've been through so much to make it to this point. You both deserve happiness."

"Thanks, Ruby," I said. "And thank you again for letting me stay with you. Jesse is on nights at the hospital, and I still get squeamish when I'm alone, especially on Full Moon night."

"Right, tonight," she sighed. "Just two more sleeps to go, then you can be wrapped up in Harper's arms again."

25

I groaned. "It can't come soon enough."

*

"I thought that we could do our nails tonight." Ruby smiled. Her pearly teeth gleamed as she set down a tray of polish and nail tools. "Well, I could do both of yours since mine don't grow any more."

Eden laughed and slid off the chesterfield couch onto the floor. "I hope that file isn't silver, Rubes."

"And why would I own a silver nail file?"

"Why would you own a file at all if your nails don't grow?"

I laughed, and Ruby shrugged.

"Good point." She grinned. "I've had it from when I was human, I guess. It's stainless steel."

"Can I go first?" Eden asked, holding her hand up. "I might just varnish them; they seem to be in shape."

Of course her nails were in shape, there was nothing about the petite redhead that was *out* of shape.

"Sure, what colour?" Ruby asked.

"Mm, black."

Ruby unscrewed the lid of the nail polish, and I reached for the file to try and curve off the silly-looking stubs at the end of my fingers. Seriously, they seemed to grow square. Why was everything of mine naturally *out* of shape?

"I'm thinking of cutting my hair," Eden said after a moment. "What do you guys think?"

Ruby frowned. "But it's so long and healthy. How short

26

were you thinking?"

"Like chin-length, short."

"That's a big decision."

"It'll grow back." Eden shrugged. "What do you think, Taylor?"

I glanced up from my nail examination. "I think you'd look nice with short hair."

"So you have any scissors, Rubes?"

"You want to cut it tonight?" Ruby frowned. "Eden, what if you change your mind?"

"It'll grow back."

My brows drew together as I tried to file my nails back. When was the last time I'd done them? They were so long and tough, it was like trying to file metal.

"I have scissors, but you'll probably have to wait until your nails are dry before you attempt it," Ruby answered.

"Wicked." Eden bounced. "You're concentrating awfully hard there, Taylor. It's not rocket science, you know."

"Thanks, I know." I mumbled. "It's just… they never used to be this strong."

"Your nails?"

"Mm."

"High calcium diet?" Eden asked.

"Not really." I frowned, stifling a yawn. As I did, I inhaled some filings and felt a sneeze coming on, my head fell forward as it came out, and the next thing I heard was Ruby's hiss.

"What?" Eden jumped.

"Silver," Ruby choked. "Where did that come from?"

I held my hands up. "Wasn't me."

"Maybe it was," Eden mumbled, sliding towards me. She grabbed my hand and looked at it. I resisted the urge to pull it away. "Are you sure the file isn't silver, Ruby?"

"Why would it be silver?" Ruby shrugged. "Silver is a soft metal."

"That's why it's mostly an alloy of 92.5% and mixed with 7.5% copper," Eden answered.

I blinked at her knowledge. I still didn't know what she did, but I guess that Shadow Weavers couldn't make a living on magic.

"What percentage of silver affects a vampire?" I asked.

"I tend to just stay away from them all." Ruby coughed, wiping her face. "Was it in the filings?"

Eden bit her lip. "Wouldn't know without testing it."

Ruby leant over and pressed her finger on the table in front of me, withdrawing her hand at lightning speed. "Yes, silver."

We all exchanged thoughtful looks.

"What time is it?" Eden asked, turning towards the grandfather clock. "Crap, nearly midnight. Cole will be too occupied to call and ask him now."

I looked to Ruby. "Does Cole know everything about everything?"

"He knows a lot." She nodded. "He's seen a lot."

"He's handy to have around."

"I've always thought so."

I pressed my lips together then suddenly felt a wave of light-headedness sweep over me. I swayed and fell back against

28

the couch, clutching at my head.

"Taylor?" Ruby asked. "Are you okay?"

"I don't… feel so…" I panted, clapping my hands over my ears. It felt like every sound around me was echoing, every tick, every whisper, every scratch. I could have sworn that I could hear a cockroach scurry on the sidewalk below us. It was incredibly overbearing.

"Taylor," Eden called. Her voice seared through my eardrum, making me want to scream.

"Make it stop!" I gasped. "Make it stop!"

"Make what stop?"

"The noise, everything, it's so *loud*," I squealed. "It's… it's…"

The pain became too much for consciousness, and I felt my eyes roll back in my head as the scene went black and the sound ceased. The human body is an incredible thing.

*

I woke to find myself in a dark room, feeling like my throat had been set alight, and my head had been trampled by a stampede of African elephants. I pushed myself up to sit and looked around me, noticing that I was in some kind of closet with no windows. Weird. How did I get here? Was I still at Ruby and Cole's place?

I rose to my feet and felt around for a light. I found a switch on the wall and mashed it with my palm. When the empty room lit up, I couldn't help but gasp. The walls were

29

covered in scratch marks, looking more like an animal had been trapped in here than an unconscious human. I tried to make sense of it, too shocked to call out or even move. As awareness seeped back to me, and adrenalin pumped through my veins, I felt a pulsing in my finger joints and dropped my head to look at them. I yelped and then began beating on the door.

"Ruby! Eden!" I shouted, feeling the scratch in my throat. "Somebody?"

The door opened, and Eden stood behind it, her expression carved in a frightening scowl.

"Oh, thank goodness," I sighed. "What on earth happened? Why am I in here? Where is here? Why are my hands covered in blood?"

Her eyes flickered down to them. "That's your blood." She leant her head inside the room. "I guess trying to claw your way out would do that."

I rubbed my head then regretted it, feeling the smudge of stickiness rub off onto my clammy skin.

"What are you talking about?"

"You don't remember?"

"Clearly not. Enlighten me."

"You went crazy, Taylor," she said slowly. "Like, literally crazy. Your eyes went all pale, and you started going after Ruby for some reason, like, trying to scratch her or something. I had to get all shadow magic on you to knock you out long enough to lock you in here."

"What? You're lying."

Her eyebrows lifted over her dark eyes. "Do I look like I

am kidding with you?"

Eden had no reason to lie to me. Plus, the evidence backing up her story spoke for itself.

"Is Ruby okay?" I frowned.

"She's okay, a little shaken." Eden shrugged. "She called Cole a little while ago. I said that I'd watch over you in case you, I don't know, snapped out of it."

"How long was I trying to get out?"

"A couple of hours or so. You must've blacked out again after that."

I shook my head in bewilderment. None of this made any sense.

"Come on, since you're clearly yourself again, you should come and get cleaned up," Eden murmured, tipping her head back.

I nodded as she led the way out through the apartment and over to an elevator. When we got in, she pressed the top floor and placed her hand on a metal plate before the lift started to move. I guessed Cole didn't like any unexpected visitors in his building.

"Is Cole coming back?" I asked. "Does he know what is going on with me?"

She shrugged. "I didn't speak to him."

I sighed. "Thanks for looking out for me."

"I was looking out for Ruby."

"Right."

For some reason, I didn't see Eden and me painting each other's nails in the near future.

31

"Taylor, are you all right?" Ruby asked as the door opened. "You're bleeding."

"I'm fine," I breathed. "How are you? I didn't hurt you did I? Eden said that I, um—"

"I'm fine, no harm done."

Eden glanced at me warily.

"Come on, I'll show you to the bathroom," Ruby said, walking me forward. "Lesleigh decked out my wardrobe, so you can help yourself to a change of clothes."

I looked down and only noticed then that my jeans were also ripped with scratch marks, four long cuts down each of my thighs, and my sweater was in tatters. Great, I guess I'll have to go shopping again.

"Ruby, what happened to me?" I whispered. "Does Cole know?"

Ruby pursed her lips then shook her head. "He's not sure; he'll have to run tests when he gets back."

"When is that?"

"Tomorrow."

"He's not coming back earlier? What if I go crazy again?"

"There is still another night for Harper to change," she replied. "And Eden will be here."

I frowned. "I don't think she likes me much."

"You did give us both a bit of a scare."

"I'm sorry."

"I told you, no harm done," she answered with a slight headshake. "I'll get you a towel so you can clean up, and if you would like to put on one of the robes in the cupboard there, then you can go and find something to wear."

"Thank you. I'm sorry for all the trouble I've caused."

"Nonsense," she breathed. "What are friends for?"

I smiled back at her. I guess I didn't know until then.

Phase Two

The Thick Skin

I drove home from Ruby's after changing and having some breakfast to drop off my uni stuff and change into my own clothes. I was also feeling pretty embarrassed and confused about how I had behaved the night before. I didn't feel dangerous at all, not as a mere human, so it bothered me a little that she, an immortal and near indestructible vampire, was concerned that maybe I could harm her.

As I pulled up at the unit that I shared with my twin brother, Jesse, I couldn't help but think about what that Italian guy Sal had said to me; that maybe I *wasn't* human or my number, or something, had expired. I still didn't know what it meant entirely, but I could only assume that whatever was wrong with me had something to do with that. After what I'd seen, it was foolish to overlook anything suspicious. After what I'd seen, I was convinced that nothing in South Coast was a coincidence.

"Where have you been?" a voice asked from my couch as I pushed open the door. I looked up and groaned internally at the tuft of blond hair and blue eyes that peered up at me.

"What are you doing here, Brandon?" I mumbled. "Jesse is on-call all weekend in the emergency department."

"I know, that's why I'm here," he replied. "He said that I could stay and study where it's quiet."

"There are places available to the public to study in silence, you know, they're called libraries."

He rolled his eyes. "Well, you haven't even been here, so I don't know why you're bothered by it."

"I'm not bothered, I just didn't expect you to be here," I muttered walking passed him to go to my room.

"What are you wearing?" he asked. "Is that new?"

I looked down at the grey maxi-dress and frowned. "It's not mine. I borrowed it from a friend."

"Looks nice on you."

"Um, thanks."

He smiled and went back to playing with my black kitten, Raven. She was getting bigger now and was so much healthier than when I'd found her under my car. She loved being around Brandon, and he seemed to love her as much as any of us. For a while, I found it hard to be around her, feeling her golden eyes watching me. The last pair of golden eyes didn't belong to something nearly as kind as a house cat, it had been the wendigo that had hunted me – the wendigo that Harper, Ruby, Cole, and Hunter had saved me from. I shivered at the thought.

Brandon's blue eyes glanced up. "So, are you hanging around? I can go if you don't want me here."

I instantly felt guilty that I'd made him feel unwelcome. He was still Jesse's best friend, and even if I had felt overlooked by him growing up, he probably didn't deserve my attitude now.

"I'm not staying so you can stay," I sighed. "You practically live here anyway."

"Where are you going?"

"Back to my friend's place."

His brow creased. "You mean April?"

"No." I frowned. April McKenzie was my best friend before I left for Europe over a year ago. We had lost touch when I was away, considering I'd gone when we weren't on the best of terms. When I returned to South Coast, I had reluctantly tried to rekindle the friendship, but apparently, I'd changed more than she had, and that change just drove a bigger wedge between us. I hadn't seen her in a few weeks, since Jesse had insisted that I have a girl's night with her and his girlfriend, Ashley. It had gone horribly, and I ended up leaving.

"Which friend? Do I know her?"

I pressed my lips together at the assumption that it was a female. I guess Brandon was still under the impression that if I didn't want him, then I didn't want to be with any guy.

"No, you don't know her," I answered. "She's someone that I know through Harper."

"Harper?" He blinked. "Oh, right. I think Jesse mentioned that he was back in the picture."

I nodded.

"I should go soon anyway, I have a date tonight," he sighed.

"Really?" I wasn't really surprised. Brandon never had trouble getting dates.

"Yup."

I turned to leave.

"We should double date sometime," he said. "Me and Millie, you and that Harper guy."

I pressed my lips together. Harper had never seemed to warm to Brandon, and he wasn't really a 'double-date' kind of guy. He was more of a lone wolf, pun intended.

"Wait, did you say Millie?" I blinked. "As in Amelia Saber? You're dating the mayor's daughter?"

Brandon grinned. "Yup."

Amelia was a year younger than we were, turning twenty-two this year, and worked for the state government with her father. I'm not sure what her actual title was, but it appeared that she was doing well in her career. Her father would be proud.

"Isn't she dating some other guy?" I asked. I didn't follow the tabloids much, but I remember seeing in the social pages that she was with someone called Marcus. He looked nice. They made a cute couple.

"Nope, not any more." He shrugged.

"And I thought you were seeing the Police Commissioner's daughter."

"Who, Isobel?" He frowned. "Nuh, I ended that. She's too high maintenance for me."

"Or too mature."

"Hey, she was only a year older than us," he replied. "And age is just a number."

"Mm."

37

Brandon stroked Raven, and I could hear her purring from where I stood. "So yeah, we should set something up."

"Maybe," I sighed, stifling a yawn. "Well, I'm just going to grab some things then head out. Lock up after you leave."

"I know the drill, Taylor." He smiled.

I nodded and continued to my room. I hadn't spent a lot of time at home since Harper had come back, mostly because the one time that we'd hung out here, Jesse was home and had almost tried to surgically remove answers from Harper. Aside from that, Brandon spent a lot of time here, and unlike Jesse, he didn't have the filter of love for me to edit himself around my new boyfriend.

I took my time at home before returning to Cole and Ruby's apartment block. When I eventually made my way back, Ruby was waiting in the garage for me.

"I was getting worried," she sighed. "But I'm glad that you're all right."

"I'm sorry. I just thought that I should do a bit of cleaning at home. I haven't really done a lot over the past week."

She smiled. "I understand, but I hope that was the only reason for you staying away."

Her eyes flickered to the quick rise and fall of my chest, and I rested my hand over my beating heart. I should have known better than to lie to a vampire.

I exhaled. "It wasn't the only reason, no. I just, I guess I was ashamed of trying to attack you, or whatever I did last night. I thought that you'd feel more comfortable if I wasn't here."

Ruby's head tipped. "Taylor, that's so silly. I know you would never hurt me on purpose. You didn't seem to be yourself when it happened, it was so strange. Besides, I promised Harper that I'd look out for you, and I always keep my word."

I pressed my lips together, and she ushered me towards the elevator. "Come on, let's get inside before nightfall."

"You really want to take the risk with me again?"

"It was one night out of two." She smiled as we stepped in the lift. "I think I'll hedge my bets."

I laughed incredulously. "I've never had a friend that risked their life for me before."

"That's not true. Aside from Harper, you have Cole and me, and even Hunter. Remember?"

"I don't know if Hunter would call me a friend," I replied. She had received some pretty severe injuries from the wendigo but, thanks to her quick-healing feline body, she lived to tell the tale. She hadn't really been thrilled to help defend me to begin with, but I suppose being hurt was the final straw. I wasn't surprised that I hadn't seen her since, but I was concerned that Ruby hadn't heard from her. Harper had told me that Hunter first came to South Coast with Ruby and Cole after they'd met her in their travels abroad. It seemed strange that she would just leave without a trace.

"So what do you have planned for tonight?" I asked. "Or is *stay alive* the only thing on the list."

Ruby laughed, and it sounded musical. "No, well yes, that's at the top. But I thought that maybe we could like do a puzzle or something, or maybe watch another movie?"

I smiled. "A puzzle, really? Are we that boring?"

"I know, it's pathetic, right?" She smirked as the elevator doors opened to her and Cole's apartment floor because the apartment was an entire floor. "But it's not like we can get drunk together, or make food, or do makeovers. What do people usually do on sleepovers? I never really had them growing up."

"You're asking me?" I blinked. "I didn't have many growing up either. Jesse and I just used to build forts and play with action figurines."

"We can build a fort." She shrugged. "I think Lesleigh has left a bunch of her material in one of the rooms."

"Lesleigh... she's the other vampire who comes and goes?"

"Yes, she's still in Spain, as far as I know, she's lovely, she's a fashion designer," Ruby answered.

"Really?"

"You've heard of Ambrosia White?"

I blinked. "No way."

"Lesleigh Ambrosia White." Ruby smiled. "I'm literally the only vampire that I know who isn't creative in any way. I mean, after a lot of practice I can play the guitar, but I can't draw to save myself."

"I guess it's lucky that you're already dead then." I shrugged, then gasped. "Wow that was rude, I'm so sorry."

Ruby laughed. "That's a good one. I'll have to use it."

I pressed my lips together. "So is Eden coming tonight?"

"Maybe. She said she might drop by later to, um, check in."

40

"You mean check up on me?"

"She means well."

"It's probably for the best." I nodded. "So, where is this material?"

Ruby grinned. "This is going to be so much fun!"

*

"Taylor," my name rang – my name in that glorious French-English accent. My eyes were closed, so I assumed that I must still be dreaming. Harper was somewhat of a star in my dreams, even if I never seemed to capture his perfection as accurately as it was in reality.

I felt my shoulder move and groaned. I didn't want to wake up if I was dreaming of Harper. I had never dreamt of his voice, his accent, so flawlessly before.

"Taylor," he said again. Thank goodness I hadn't lost it. I felt myself smile, then felt something warm press to my lips, warm and soft. Wow, my imagination was really – wait!

My eyes shot open, and I gasped before throwing myself at him, sending him flying back against the material of the fort that Ruby and I had built.

"You're back," I gasped. "I thought that I was dreaming, but then I realised that my imagination sucks!"

Harper chuckled, moving his arms right around me. "I missed you."

"I missed you too," I sighed. "So much."

"Taylor?" Ruby's voice said. Oops, I'd almost forgotten

that we weren't alone, and we were in fact in a place with two vampires with perfect hearing. This isn't awkward.

Harper tipped his head back as I looked up, then scrambled to my feet. He took a moment and then did the same.

"Hi, I'm… yes?" I stuttered.

Ruby smiled. "You're awake."

"Mm-hm."

"Cole wanted to see you, to ask to you about the other night," she said. "When you're ready, of course."

"Oh, okay, sure."

Harper put his arm around my waist, and I straightened. It still felt weird to have someone touch me, even if I wanted him to. I guess the insecurities of being overweight for so long never really left me. The phantom feelings were still there, still reminding me that I wasn't as slim as some of the other girls.

"Why don't we let her have breakfast first before we start the interrogation?" Harper suggested.

I looked up at him and bit my lip.

"I'm sorry, I didn't mean for it to sound like an interrogation," Ruby answered. "I sometimes forget about human needs. Please, Taylor, come, and I'll prepare you something."

I nudged Harper playfully. "He didn't mean that. Harper is just a bit protective of me. I'm happy to talk whenever. I'm actually a little curious to hear what theories Cole has about what happened."

Cole took my blood pressure as I waited for Ruby and Harper to cook me breakfast. I'd offered to do it myself, but

Ruby wouldn't allow it as a host, and Harper just wanted to care for me. I gave up arguing with the two of them, and instead, let Cole do his doctor-thing. I wasn't a stranger to all things medical, considering my father, Jackson Mistry, was a doctor at one of South Coast's largest hospitals, plus my twin Jesse was also studying medicine. I suppose it interested me too in a way, but I took more of an interest in animals and, after studying animal science for a year, I was now in my fourth year of veterinary science. I also tried to help when I could at one of the local vet clinics.

"Are you feeling all right, Taylor?" Cole asked. "Your heart rate is a little high."

I dropped my gaze from Harper and felt my cheeks burn.

"Sorry, I'm feeling fine."

Cole looked between us and chuckled. "I see."

"So what's next?" I asked. "Do you need a blood sample?"

Ruby and Harper turned to stare at me.

"To test my blood. I'm not offering myself up as breakfast, relax," I sighed.

Cole was smirking as he removed a syringe from his medical kit. "That might help, yes. The sample, not the breakfast."

I laughed and rolled up my sleeve. "You might need a butterfly needle, my veins are temperamental."

"I'm sure it'll be fine," he answered, pressing the point to the inside of my elbow. I felt pressure and looked down at it.

"What's wrong?"

"You seem to have thick skin, Taylor," he mused. "Quite

43

literally. It doesn't seem to want to be broken."

"Are you kidding? I stab myself with my nails all the time, and it bleeds."

Cole shuffled towards me and reached for a scalpel. "May I try something, Taylor?"

I shrugged.

"What are you doing, Cole?" Harper's panicked voice asked.

"I am testing whether her skin *is* breakable."

"You're going to cut her?"

The point of the blade had already pressed against the side of my arm. It wouldn't bleed much if it did break the skin... *if.*

"How curious." The male vampire frowned. "I have never encountered anything like it before. If I couldn't smell your human scent or hadn't seen you bleed before, then I might think that you were something other than human."

I blinked. "It's funny that you should say that."

"Funny how?" Harper asked, suddenly at my side.

"Well, there was this guy on Friday at uni who said something... something about me not being human. He asked what I was, and then said that I had a strange vibe or something."

"Vibe? He said that?" Cole asked. "Can you remember his name?"

"His name was Sal. Salvatore something. Um, Vin... Vincenzo, I mean, Vincent," I stuttered. "Salvatore Vincent."

He nodded and suddenly his phone was at his ear.

"What are you doing?"

"Making a call to someone who has access to the university records to see when he has class next."

"Why?"

"Perhaps this Salvatore knows something about you that we don't."

"How would he...?" I sighed. "He... he's studying philosophy if that makes a difference."

Harper's hand moved around my shoulder. "How did you meet him if he is studying philosophy?"

"The library. I had to photocopy some readings, and he kept staring at me, and then followed me out while I waited for Ruby," I replied as Harper's arms tightened around me.

"I'm sorry that I wasn't there to protect you."

"He was harmless. He just sort of freaked me out a bit." I shrugged. "He asked if I had died. He said something about my number being up."

"Your number?" Harper frowned. "Your life number?"

Cole looked up. "He has a lecture on Monday morning, and also happens to live in the student housing. Tomorrow I think that we should have a chat with young Mr Vincent and see what he has to say."

"Um, why don't you just let me?" I said. "He seemed interested in talking to me, so maybe it will look less suspicious if I ask him questions than to have a few of us approach him."

Cole looked like he wanted to disagree with me, but didn't verbalise it. Actually, it was Harper who gave voice to his disapproval.

"No, not on your own," he replied. "I will come with you."

"Harper—"

"Taylor, if he has been asking these sorts of questions, then he clearly knows something about our world," Harper explained. "You do not know the types of questions to ask to receive the right answers about what we are dealing with."

I bit my lip. "I was just going to say 'Harper, I took it as a given that you'd be with me'."

His face softened into a smile. "Oh."

"Until then, I don't think that we should worry," Cole said, looking like he didn't quite believe his own advice. "If it was only the one evening, then it could be nothing."

"So why can't my skin be broken then?"

Cole's hand rested on my shoulder. "It is probably a good thing that your body is protecting itself. Perhaps it is a side-effect of living through what you did."

"Some side-effect. I guess it means that I won't be getting the flu shot this year."

"Breakfast." Ruby smiled, putting the scrambled eggs down in front of me. "I hope it's to your liking."

"It was yesterday, *and* the day before," I replied, scratching a tickle on my arm as I spoke. "You're too kind, thank you so much for everything, Ruby. Especially after, you know."

"Hold on." Cole frowned, reaching for my hand. He turned my fingers up and examined them. He moved his hand over the top of my nails and then recoiled.

"What did I do?" I frowned.

"Nothing." Cole blinked. "But there appears to be silver in the nail fibres."

46

"Silver?"

"The nail file," Ruby mused. "Taylor, you were filing your nails before you sneezed the other night. You must have blown the dust at me."

I rubbed my head. "This is absolutely crazy. I don't know what's going on here, but it's all completely ridiculous."

Harper's fingers brushed my cheeks, but I couldn't smile. If I had silver in me, that meant that I could repel him the same way that made Cole recoil.

"It will be fine, we'll get some answers," Harper sighed. "Just eat your breakfast; nothing can be done about it right now."

"How can you be so calm? If I have silver in me, that means I could hurt you too."

Harper slipped onto the seat beside me. "It also means that *I* cannot hurt *you*. Nothing supernatural can. That at least gives me some relief."

I gazed at his glorious face and watched how the love in his olive green eyes seemed to make them glow. Whatever I had to go through to lead me to him was worth it. I would do it again, I would face death again just to be able to have him look at me the way he was in that moment. He leant over, pressing his perfectly carved lips to my forehead.

"Eat, Taylor," he murmured. "Then we can go to our own world for a while, and worry about what all of this means tomorrow."

I nodded and glanced down at the eggs. I didn't feel hungry, but I knew that I needed to eat. Ruby passed me a fork,

47

and I moved closer to the table, but not before catching a wary look that Cole discretely gave to Harper.

I didn't know what any of it meant for me, and I certainly didn't know what it would mean for me and Harper, or us, or my other friends. But I did know that right now, whatever it was, it was worrying the three of them more than they were letting on.

*

Harper and I left shortly after I insisted on helping with the clearing away of the dishes and the material fort. We went to his place rather than mine since I knew that around now Jesse would be pouring into bed after the long stint at the hospital. I didn't know how he did it, but he was pretty amazing to work the hours that he did and still keep up a social life with his friends like Brandon, and his girlfriend, Ashley.

Harper had moved into Hunter's cottage after she had left, or rather disappeared. It was east of the city and fringed by the Stanley Colvin State Park, so a beautiful location for someone who enjoyed seclusion and nature. South Coast was pretty small by way of cities, but some pockets were a little more isolated than others. It definitely was a step up from him staying with his godfather, Rob, and his family, Ebony, Eden, and her brothers, but that didn't mean that I necessarily enjoyed the fact that we seemed to spend most of our time together in the place that held the rawest memories for me. It was the place that we had used as a base to lure the wendigo to us, where it found us, and nearly killed Hunter and me. It was the place where Harper had almost killed me, and then was nearly killed by the banshee. It was the place where he had told me that he was leaving to keep us both safe. Now that he was back and we were together, it didn't seem so bad, but that didn't mean that the memories didn't still keep me up at night.

"You're not still worrying about this, are you, Taylor?" Harper asked as he cuddled up to me on the couch that had once been his deathbed.

"A bit."

"You can't change it by worrying," he whispered, dipping his lips to my neck. "Neither of us can, so please put it out of your mind for now."

I caught his face in my hands. "Harper, this could be serious."

"Or it could be trivial."

"I don't want to hurt you."

"I take the same risk with you every day."

I pouted. "Not every day."

"I'm still stronger than the average human," he answered, lifting an eyebrow.

"Bragger." I smiled as his lips sank to mine. I felt his heat through my entire body; his heartbeat was so strong and vital that it shook me as it thumped against my chest. My body ached for every part of him, but for some stupid reason, all I could hear was Eden's voice in my mind. *"I can't believe that you're a unicorn. I bet Harper isn't, he is an animal after all."*

I froze beneath him and exhaled.

"Something wrong?" he panted.

"No, not—" I bit my lip. "It's just…"

Harper sat up and tipped his head. His floppy auburn hair was sticking up at all angles. It had grown out a bit since I'd first met him. He could tuck the front of it behind his ears now.

"It's stupid really." I laughed. "You're going to think, well, I don't know what you'll think."

"Taylor, please just tell me. Then I will tell you what I think."

I swallowed nervously.

"I guess, I was just wondering if you've ever…?" I began and then stopped. How was I supposed to ask my boyfriend if he was a virgin or not? How was I supposed to deal with my insecurities when he tells me that he's not? Because of course he isn't. He's a hot-blooded twenty-eight-year-old werewolf. I instantly regretted even thinking the question.

"Have I ever what?" he asked. His brow creased as his hand moved up to rest over my collarbone. "Why are you so nervous?"

I breathed a slightly hysterical laugh. "I'm… I'm not nervous."

He smirked at the lie.

"I don't know, this is all new to me," I sighed.

"What is?"

"Being in a couple, and everything that goes with it."

"Ah," he exhaled, shuffling against me. "You want to know how many other girls I have been with."

"How… how many?" I stuttered. "Like, there's more than

one?"

I thought that I saw Harper blush a little, but I couldn't talk, my face felt like the inside of a furnace.

"Well, *how many* are there?"

His green eyes blinked. "Were there."

"Whatever."

"Taylor," he murmured. "This conversation is not one that will end well. The past is the past, *you* are my future."

I looked to the side as I considered that as a satisfying answer. As a sane, rational person, it was the best answer that I could hope for, but as a paranoid and insecure female, it didn't even brush the surface.

"Are there that many?" I pouted. "Is that why you won't tell me?"

"No. But I know you, and I know that you already compare yourself to every other girl out there. I don't want to give faces to those demons."

"Demons." I muttered. "Now that you've said that it only makes it worse. I'm a scientist, I look for answers, and you being all philosophical is just frustrating."

He pulled me against him, and I rested my head on his shoulder.

"I'm sorry that I frustrate you."

"You don't, those demons do," I mumbled.

"I love *you*, Taylor."

"I love you too. But I wasn't the first one to love you."

"You will be the last."

I shook my head. "No, you're loveable. You're like a giant

51

puppy. People love puppies."

He chuckled. "You're the only one that I want."

I looked up at him and my eyes glazing over the healed puncture holes where the banshee had sunk her nails into him. His godfather, Rob, had cured him with his blood, but the scars remained even though he usually healed from regular cuts. Harper said that when he was wounded with silver, and if it was severe enough, a scar remained when it repaired. It must be the same for supernatural attacks too. The four scratch marks that I had received when I had been marked by the banshee had healed when the banshee who marked me had died. Sometimes I wished that I still had a scar to show from the battle that we all fought like Harper did. But the scars merely existed in my memory.

"I'm sorry that I'm so damaged and self-doubting," I whispered. "Sometimes I still don't feel like I'm quite enough, and I'm scared that, because I love you so much, if you were to leave me again, even though I was alone before, I wouldn't know how to be alone any more. I know that it's unhealthy to think that way, but it feels like you're a part of me now, like a part of who I am, and that's really scary."

"It's scary for me too," he replied. "But you are enough, Taylor, you always have been, and I'm not going anywhere."

I nodded.

"So please do not be jealous of ghosts," he murmured, dropping his lips to the side of my head. "And as for the rest, *being a couple and the stuff that goes with it*, we can figure that out as we go. It's just you and me, so we can do as little, or as much as you are comfortable with."

"It's not that I'm not comfortable with you." I blushed. "It's more that I don't really know what I'm doing."

"There are no rules." He smiled weakly. "Only instincts."

I frowned as Eden's voice played on repeat: "*he is an animal after all.*"

Harper's thumb brushed over the corner of my down-turned lips. "What did I say?"

"Not you, just something someone else said."

"Who?"

"Eden?"

"Eden?" he asked. "Rob's daughter?"

"Mm."

"Whatever she said, she doesn't know what she's talking about."

"It just sounded like she did." I shrugged. "That's why it bothered me."

He frowned.

"Just forget that I said anything," I sighed. "Like you said, it's just you and me, and we can do whatever we want."

"No pressure." He nodded. "Deal?"

"Okay, deal," I whispered.

His nose ran down my jaw, and I lifted my head to kiss him, setting the nerve endings in my body on fire again. His hands dropped, and if I weren't so captivated, I would have felt more panicky that he could feel the contours of my body that I was still paranoid about. But I was captivated by him, and every touch just twisted his body closer to mine. It was thrilling and terrifying at the same time.

"Harper," I gasped.

"Taylor," he sighed.

"I need to study."

He panted for breath between kisses. "Right now?"

"Soon," I murmured against his lips. "I haven't... I'm a bit behind because of... because..."

I sighed as his sweltering lips moved across to my neck. My heart felt like it was going to rupture, and my ears started ringing. Wait, no, that was actual ringing. I opened my eyes and reached for my bag. Harper exhaled as he sat back to allow me to move.

"I'm sorry," I breathed.

Harper nodded.

I drew in a breath and hit answer. "Jesse."

"Tay, hey." My brother yawned. *"Where are you? Have you been home this week at all?"*

"Uh, I'm out. I was home yesterday when Brandon was there sprawled out on our couch," I replied. "Why?"

"No reason. I was just worried, you're usually a homebody, well, you were until... oh, you're with Harper, right?"

"Yes."

"Okay. Will you be home later? I was going to chuck a roast on to cook, or something. Harper is welcome too. Ash is coming and, you know, Brandon will probably be here."

I frowned and looked at Harper who could probably hear everything that Jesse was saying. His bright green eyes were watching me patiently. He was leaving it up to me to decide whether I subjected him to my twin, his moody girlfriend, and his obnoxious best friend. I really wanted to see Jesse, and I really wanted to stay with Harper, but I didn't know if I wanted those two worlds to collide just yet. I suppose they would need to eventually.

"Taylor? You still there?" Jesse asked.

"I'm here," I murmured. "And I'll be home later."

Harper's eyes dropped.

"Um, Harper will be there too," I added. "We'll be there together."

"Really?" Jesse's voice seemed to lift. *"Okay, cool. See you both later then."*

"Bye, Jess."

I dropped the phone from my ear, and Harper looked up.

"We'll be there together," he said.

"Yes. Is that okay?"

"Yes."

"Really?"

"Yes." Harper smiled. "Jesse is important to you. I think that it's time we start to get to know each other, considering neither of us are going anywhere."

I beamed. "No, you're not."

"But as for the other guy."

"Ugh, Brandon, I know," I groaned. "Even Ashley. I love my brother, but sometimes I seriously question the company he keeps."

"He could possibly think the same for you."

"No, he wouldn't think that. I have the best company."

Harper's eyebrow lifted. "So he would be okay with the fact that you're dating a werewolf, had a sleepover with a vampire, and have also been known to hang out with shape-shifting were-panthers, and those gifted with black magic?"

"Shadow magic."

"That makes it okay?"

"Jesse would be happy as long as I am happy." I shrugged. "He's felt a lot of the pain that I have over the years. It's a twin thing."

"So if he doesn't like me?" Harper asked.

I sighed. "Then we'd be about even when it came to fondness for the other's partners."

*

"So, Harper, where did you disappear to?" Brandon asked as Harper, and I sat down on one side of the couch. Brandon took up the whole other side on his own.

Harper glanced over at him. "Disappear?"

"You bailed on Tay for a while, didn't you?"

"I wouldn't put it quite like that."

"How would you put it?"

I glared at Brandon. "Harper had some personal things to attend to."

"Really? Well, it would have been nice for him to tell you that."

"What do you even know about it anyway?"

Brandon shrugged. "Well, *I* didn't leave."

Jesse walked over and punched his friend in the arm. "Shut up and help me set the table."

I sighed and leant into Harper. "Sorry."

He just gave a slight shake of his head.

"So where's, um, Ashley?" I asked, more out of courtesy than curiosity. "I thought that she would be here."

Harper lifted a finger, and there was a knock at the door.

"Oh," I breathed, and couldn't help but smile.

I half turned when Jesse opened the door to his girlfriend of a couple of years. Her just-below shoulder-length dark red hair was flattened straight, as per usual, and her brown eyes were decorated with eye-shadow and liner which somehow seemed to make her look natural, despite the artificial element involved. Ashley always looked as if she was ready to go clubbing, or step into a wedding party because she was a beauty therapist. I wasn't quite sure how someone who painted makeup and waxed someone else qualified as any kind of therapist, but admittedly, I was a bit of a moron when it came to anything beauty-related. My idea of skin treatment was washing my face in the morning and not piling on layers of foundation. Lucky for me, my skin allowed me to boycott any more effort than that.

"Ash, this is Harper, Taylor's, um, boyfriend," Jesse said, walking her around in front of us. "Harper, this is Ashley, my girlfriend."

Harper's face broke into the most heart melting smile. "Ashley, Taylor has mentioned you, it's a pleasure."

Ashley blinked and then breathed a laugh. "Oh, um, I... it's

57

a pleasure to meet you too. What kind of accent is that?"

"English," Harper answered. "With a little French mixed in."

"French, wow, you're from… is that how you met? When Taylor was in France?"

I noticed how she didn't talk directly to me. I guess even though my boyfriend impressed her a little, she clearly still wasn't over the lack of effort that I'd made to impress her over the years.

"No, we never crossed paths when Taylor was abroad," he replied. "Though I did recognise her when I transferred here. I had seen her in Rome when I went there one weekend."

Ashley exhaled. "That's so romantic."

My eyebrows lifted as Brandon's face crumbled.

"Romantic?" He huffed. "If he'd have recognised her from a weekend in Almanbury it wouldn't be romantic. Just because it's Europe, everyone swoons."

Jesse laughed. "I'm going to start serving soon, so if you want to find a place at the table, then we can get started."

Brandon sauntered over and flopped into a seat. I contemplated sitting on the other side of the table, but then knew that it would mean that Harper would have to sit beside him, so I slipped in the chair next to him.

"Hey there." Brandon grinned.

I rolled my eyes and took Harper's hand as he sat down on my other side.

"So, Harper, what part of France are you from?" Ashley pressed, sitting on his other side. I only just realised that I

58

didn't even know that. I'd always assumed that it was Paris since that's where he first encountered me. Why would he otherwise have been in such a big city if he wasn't from there? Harper wasn't one to willingly hang out in a crowded place.

"My mother was from Brittany, it's west and a little south of Paris," he replied. "I spent some time growing up there, from when I was about four until I was twelve. Then we moved back to Derbyshire, where I was born."

I squeezed Harper's hand, and he looked over at me, smiling weakly. I could feel the questions in my eyes and wondered if he could see them. He leant over to kiss me on the cheek.

"So why come to South Coast? It's not exactly a place I'd expect someone to pass up Europe for."

He smiled at me. "It has its attractions."

Ashley exhaled. "You're so lucky, Taylor."

"I know."

"Ugh, God this is insufferable," Brandon groaned. "If I'd known that the dinner came with couples-strings, I would have—"

"What?" I asked. "Gone where?"

He shrugged. "Somewhere else."

"You have nowhere else."

"I have a home, Taylor."

"Really? Do you remember where it is?"

Brandon sighed. "So sue me if I prefer to hang out here with my friends."

"Friends?"

"You know, words can wound, Taylor," he replied.

I rolled my eyes.

"Amelia couldn't come tonight then, Brandon?" Ashley asked. It was honestly the most I'd heard her talk without venom in her tone, ever.

He wrinkled his freckled nose. "Nuh, she does Sunday dinners with her family."

I smirked. "Because the mayor has such a great family life."

"At least they make an effort," Brandon muttered.

"Dinner is served," Jesse said, setting the sliced beef on the table. "I hope no one is vegetarian."

Harper and I both laughed. "No."

"Excellent."

"Looks good, darling." Ashley smiled.

Darling.

"I hope it tastes okay." Jesse frowned. "I was just chucking in whatever we had to flavour it."

"It smells great," Harper replied, brushing his cutlery. I saw him flinch and tipped my head at the silver laid in front of us.

"Jess, are we using the good, um, silverware?"

Jesse shrugged. "Yeah, I thought that we would since it's a special occasion."

I breathed a laugh that sounded flat. "It's not really. Can't we just use the stainless steel stuff?"

"It's already out, Taylor."

"I know, but—"

"Who cares?" Brandon asked, stabbing a slice of beef off the serving plate and shoving it in his mouth. "It works the

60

same."

I scratched my head. "Well, I care, because Harper is allergic to silver."

"Allergic?" Jesse frowned. "I've never heard of that before."

"He gets this rash when he—ouch!" I yelped, resting my hand on my fork.

Harper jumped back. "Taylor? Are you all right? What happened? Are you okay?"

The urgency in his voice wasn't foreign to me, but I could see the same questioning expression reflected on the other three faces at the table.

"Yes, it was just hot. It must've been warmed by the roast plate." I exhaled, tentatively sliding my knife off the table. It felt a little warm and tingly on my skin, like the time I had spilt hydrochloric acid on myself during an experiment. Though, it didn't seem to sizzle like I'd heard when Harper or Ruby touched it. I collected Harper's cutlery and mine and took them to the kitchen to replace them with the regular steel ones that we usually used.

"Sorry, Harper, I had no idea," Jesse was saying when I returned. "Taylor hasn't told me much about you, which is partly why I wanted to have you over."

"I haven't told you, Jess, because Harper is a private person," I answered.

"It's okay, Taylor." Harper smirked. "I'm sure that your brother just wants to make sure that I am good enough for you."

61

I scoffed. "Of course you are. You're the best for me."

"He doesn't know that, and I can see that he's as protective of you as I am."

Jesse nodded, a smile playing on his lips. "What he said."

"I understand, Jesse, you don't know me, and neither Taylor nor I have given you the opportunity to know me. But let me assure you that I am completely committed to her happiness and safety," Harper said, resting his hand on mine. "I know that my sudden disappearance before caused her pain, and the thought haunts me every day. However, I'm back now, for good, and I will prove to you and to Taylor that her letting me back into her life was not a mistake."

I smiled weakly. "Not a mistake."

Jesse pulled in his lower lip. "Okay. I'll let you prove it, but just know that Taylor is a private person too, so if she's chosen to trust you, never take advantage of that. I was here when you left, I saw what that did to her, and I don't want to *ever* see her like that again. If you hurt my sister, you hurt me, and unlike her, I won't take it lying down."

Silence fell upon the table.

Brandon stared at the peas on his plate, Ashley examined her cuticles, and my brother and Harper met each other with an even stare. I had stopped breathing.

"I understand," Harper said after an eternal few seconds. "And I will never hurt her again. You have my word."

"Well, okay then." Jesse nodded. "Let's eat."

Phase Three

The Grim Truth

After dinner, Harper and I walked in silence out to his Honda Shadow motorbike. The conversation had seemed to lighten up after Jesse's brotherly warning, and Harper seemed to fit in with my human, well, friends as well as I did.

"I'm sorry about Jesse," I said as we reached the black and silver bike. "He's just worried."

"I know," Harper answered. "I expected him to be. It needed to be said."

I reached my arms around his waist and hugged him. "Thanks for being so wonderful."

"I meant what I said."

"I know."

"I will always protect you as best I can," he replied. "No matter what comes our way."

I drew in a ragged breath at the reminder of the confusion that still surrounded what was happening to me.

"The silver cutlery, it sort of tingled my skin when I touched it," I said. "I didn't exactly burn, but it felt weird."

Harper frowned. "Something curious is definitely going on.

Hopefully, we will find out more tomorrow."

I nodded.

"I almost forgot, I got you something." He smiled.

"Me? What for? What is it?"

He laughed, reaching inside his leather jacket and pulling out something white hanging on a black cord. A wolf tooth.

"You're giving me your dad's tooth?" I blinked. "But you never take that off."

"Not my father's, mine," he said, stepping around to fasten it around my neck. "I lost it last change, and Cole collected it for me. It's a little unconventional by way of a jewellery gift, but it's something to remind you of me."

I looked down at it and smiled. "I can't believe that's yours, it's huge."

"Yes, well…"

"Did you lose a human tooth because you lost a wolf tooth?" I asked. "Is that how it works?"

"No, wolves have more teeth than humans, ten more to be exact, so there is no difference to my human set," he answered. "But I don't need to educate you on animal anatomy."

I nodded and rested my hands on his neck to reach up and kiss him. I could feel his heart accelerate, and was thrilled that it was me who had that effect on him. My grip tightened, curling my fingers, and I felt Harper's breath catch against my lips. I stepped back and frowned.

"Sorry," he breathed. "Your nails, they…"

My heart sank. "Oh, I'm sorry. Maybe I should start wearing gloves."

He reached out and caught my hand, pressing his lips to my skin. "No, you're perfect."

I tried to smile, but failed. Whatever was happening to me was affecting our relationship. The sooner we found out, the better, and hopefully, the quicker that we could fix it.

"I'll come by and pick you up in the morning," he murmured, cupping my face with his palm. "Sleep well, fair Taylor."

"You know one of these days maybe… maybe you won't have to leave at night time." I shrugged, resting my hand on his. "Maybe you could stay with me, and we can sleep beside each other."

He smiled. "I'd like that very much."

"Thank you again for coming tonight, it meant a lot to me."

"You're welcome."

I turned my head to kiss his palm. "I love you."

"I love you too," he whispered. "To the Moon and back."

"I'll see you tomorrow morning."

"Sunrise can't come soon enough."

*

I tapped my foot impatiently as Harper, and I waited outside the philosophy building on Monday morning. I was missing the end of my early class, but that wasn't what made me so nervous. It was the inevitable conversation that would come as soon as Sal's class finished.

"What if he's skipping class today?" I asked Harper,

checking my watch. Most lectures and tutorials finished fifteen minutes early to allow for travel between them. It was already after half-past nine, and the thought that he might not even be here today had only just occurred to me. Not all students considered it a necessity to attend in the final week before the exam break.

"Be patient, Taylor," Harper said calmly. "He might have just gotten caught up."

I drew in a deep breath as the door flew open, and froze mid-exhale. A sea of faces poured out the door, and I craned my head to find Sal's amongst them. Sure enough, near the back of the pack, I spotted his mass of black hair.

"Sal," I called. "Hey, Sal!"

He stopped and pivoted, letting the people pass him, and then began making his way towards where I was standing.

"Taylor. Taylor Mistry, right?" Sal smirked, his orange eyes tracing to Harper who stood beside me. His black eyebrow lifted. "And what are you?"

Harper's olive-green eyes narrowed. "I'm Harper."

"It's a pleasure, Harper, but that's not what I asked."

My mouth fell open, and Harper frowned.

"That's not why we're here," I said. "I wanted to talk to you… to ask you something."

"Is it about philosophy?" he asked. "Are you considering a change in major?"

"No."

Sal looked back to Harper, his eyes narrowing a little. "My guess is that you're either a panther or a wolf, and since that is indeed in a wolf tooth attached to the cord around your neck, I'm going to take a stab at werewolf."

Harper blinked. "Who are you?"

"Sal." He smiled. "Salvatore Vincent."

"And how do you know what I am?"

"The same way that I know she's not fully human either." Sal shrugged. "I can feel it in your vibe, your energy. It's all wrong for a human."

"If I'm not human, then what do you think I am?" I asked. "What *vibe* do I have?"

"I can't quite pick it." He frowned. "You didn't bite her did you, Wolfie? That might explain it if she was in transition."

"No, I did not," Harper growled.

"Never? Not in the heat of the moment, maybe you were nuzzling at her neck, and your teeth got a little close and—"

"Stop!" I exclaimed. "He said no."

Sal pressed his lips together. "Curious."

He turned and started to walk away.

"Wait, where are you going?" I called, trotting after him. "You haven't answered my question."

"And you never answered mine."

"What question?"

He stopped and turned, and I nearly ran into him.

"Have you ever died?"

I shrugged. "I... I drowned when I was six."

He shook his head. "No, you didn't."

"I stopped breathing, my father had to—"

"Didn't take," he interrupted shortly. "What about

recently? Did you have a brush with death and maybe lived to tell the tale?"

"She was marked," Harper answered. I looked up and saw that he was thoughtful, as if he was actually taking Sal seriously.

Sal's brow creased. "Marked?"

"It was a graze… a couple of scratches," I answered. "And it doesn't even count because I'm unmarked now."

"Marked by what?" Sal asked Harper, ignoring me.

"A banshee."

Sal blinked. "Ah, yes of course, *that's* what you are."

I felt my forehead crease. "No… no *I'm* not one, I was marked by one."

Sal sighed. "How did I miss it?"

"Because you're wrong!"

"Maybe it's because…" Sal reached out for my hand, and I pulled it away.

"What are you doing?"

"Please, Taylor. Taylor Mistry, humour me." He smirked.

I looked at Harper who had appeared to be a pensive statue, which was almost fitting considering we were still standing near philosophy building. Sal snatched at my hand again, and I smacked it.

"Trust me," he sighed.

"Why should I?"

"No reason, I guess, but no reason not to either. You can trust that I won't tell anyone about *his* little secret though. I take it you don't want every hunter in South Coast coming after you, Wolfie?"

68

"Discretion would be appreciated," Harper said slowly, his voice coming out as a low growl.

"His name is Harper," I said.

"I heard." Sal smiled. It made me angry. "Now give me your hands, Taylor."

"Why?"

Sal exhaled. "I can walk away. This clearly affects your life more than mine, but if you want answers—"

"Fine," I sneered, slapping my hands into his. "Just quit being such a wise-guy and get on with it."

"*Attractive, wise* – how you flatter me, Miss Mistry," he said.

I gritted my teeth then felt a strange feeling of calm, complacency, and clarity wash over me, moving from my hands, up my arms and through my entire body. As it reached my shoulders, though, it suddenly turned into the harshest pain that I'd ever felt, and that was saying something. I squealed and tore my hands away from him as his orange eyes scrutinised my reaction.

"What did you do to me?" I cried as the pain clustered into one spot behind my left shoulder.

Harper already had him gripped by the scruff of his shirt. I could hear the sizzle of Harper's skin against Sal's silver chain, which from it hung a sizeable silver cross. Harper didn't flinch.

"The scratches." Sal choked. "Check where you were scratched."

I didn't understand what he meant until the throbbing of my shoulder reminded me, and then I was peeling back my top to see that the four scratch marks where I'd been marked with

69

by the banshee just over twelve weeks ago were glowing red.

"What are you?" Harper growled. "What did you do?"

"I took what should have been taken the moment she was marked," Sal answered, breaking free from Harper's hold. "I took her human suffering – the kind that happens before death."

"Suffering?" I blinked. "I wasn't suffering. Haven't you been keeping up? I *didn't die*."

"But you shouldn't have lived," Sal said. "Any supernatural creature wouldn't have survived a banshee, but *you* were human, which meant that being marked put you in a kind of human purgatory where you either die as a human, or you turn."

"Turn into what? A banshee?"

Sal's black eyebrows lifted. "Like I said – *that's what you are*."

I shook my head. "No, I'm not."

"You are, Taylor."

"How?"

"Well, my guess is you killed it," he said. "The one that marked you."

I frowned. "How did you know that?"

"Because its essence was transferred into you – the nearest human, the one with its mark," he answered. "It was passed on to you."

"I think I would know if I was a banshee," I said trying to control the annoyance that was becoming louder in my voice. I looked to Harper for support, but he wasn't moving, so I turned back to Sal to defend myself. "Harper would have

70

known too. I'm not white, I don't scream, and it's simply not possible."

Sal huffed. "Not any more possible than the fact that you're dating a werewolf?"

I swallowed, gritting my teeth.

"And you wouldn't know because, from what I know of banshees, when they're in transition, they're unconscious when the change happens on the first three Full Moons," he added. "After the three Full Moons, you'll become a full screaming white-woman. Well, a banshee, because you seem to already have the screaming white-woman act down."

"You are such a jerk," I snapped.

"Did you say that she's not conscious during the first three?" Harper asked. I'd almost forgotten that he was there, he'd been so quiet for so long.

"Yes, why? Did you two lose some quality time on Friday night?"

"I wasn't with her," he answered. "I was concerned with my own turning."

"Ah, right," Sal sighed.

"Taylor, Ruby mentioned that you passed out after saying that you heard voices," Harper murmured.

Sal's eyebrow rise. "Voices?"

"They were loud, and they hurt." I nodded. "The pain made me lose consciousness. Then I woke up in that cupboard that Eden locked me in; the one that I tried to claw my way out of."

Sal exhaled loudly. "Well, case solved. You're in transition."

71

My head snapped towards him. "How do you even know about this?"

"My guess." Harper smirked. "Considering that you don't *smell* like a human, is that you are supernatural too, and judging by the way that you took away the suffering she'd feel before death, I'd say that you're a grim."

Sal smiled. "In the flesh."

"What?" I squeaked. "A grim? Like grim reaper?"

"Yeah, don't believe everything you read about us on the internet," he answered. "We're not skeletons in black cloaks. Although, I do own a black cloak, but it was for a Halloween costume."

"The fact that you're a reaper doesn't explain why you know so much about banshees specifically."

"Doesn't it?" he asked. "I reap humans who are close to death, banshees reap supernatural creatures whose numbers are up. You and I are practically a match made in death-heaven."

I frowned, and Sal sighed.

"No, the truth is I used to know a banshee, she told me a bit about them," he murmured. "I lost touch with her a while back though. Maybe she was the one you killed."

I swallowed, feeling a fleeting pinch of guilt. It was fleeting because it was a kill or be killed situation. It was watch the banshee die or watch Harper die. It wasn't even a choice. I felt no remorse.

"So three Full Moons before she turns completely?" Harper asked, ignoring Sal's comment.

"Three." Sal nodded. "How many have passed since she

killed it?"

"Two," Harper replied without missing a beat. "The second just passed."

"From what I know, it gets worse for you each time." He shrugged. "The first Full Moon Taylor probably didn't notice anything at all because that was just an activating one. The second, well, she felt what that was like last Friday. The third apex is the one that activates the final change, and from that one, every subsequent Full Moon her cry will be heard by the supernatural beings that have outlived their stay on Earth. That's when she will hunt them, and that's when she marks them and, well, screams."

Harper and I exchanged a glance, and I saw the same fear in his eyes that I felt throughout my entire body.

"If only two have passed then there's still time," Sal said, slicing the tension.

I looked over at him, gripping to the hope in his words. "Time for what? To save me?"

"Save? There's no changing back, Taylor," he answered earnestly. "What's done can't be undone, killing death has consequences."

"So what's the time for?" I sighed impatiently.

"There's time to get your werewolf boyfriend, and any other supernatural friends that you may have, as far away from you as possible. That is if they have any desire to continue walking this earth."

*

"He could be making it all up," I offered as Harper paced around Ruby and Cole's apartment. Cole stood with one arm folded across his chest, and the fingers of his other hand pressed to his lips.

"It did not sound like he was making any of it up," Harper replied quietly. "He knew a lot about it."

"Which is a little dubious in itself."

I looked over to Ruby and saw that she was as frozen as Cole was; only she looked more worried than the male vampire.

"It all certainly seems to make sense," Cole said after a moment. "I have never known a banshee personally, but from what I know *of* them and *about* them, it makes sense that Taylor…"

"So you're all going to disappear again then?" I frowned, staring at my hands. "Get as far away from me as possible, like Sal suggested?"

There was a silence that ripped at my heart, and then I saw Harper's hands appear in front of me and rest on mine.

"No," he murmured. "I told you that I'm not going anywhere, and I meant it."

Cole frowned. "But, Harper, do you—?"

"No," he repeated. "I am not leaving her again. If it's my time, then I die. Such is fate."

"Such is death," I breathed. "I don't want to be the one to kill you."

"Being apart would kill us both in a different way."

Ruby was shaking her head. "Isn't there anything else that

74

we can do to help her, Cole? I won't accept that Taylor just has to endure this."

"We all have accepted the hand that we have been dealt, Ruby." Cole frowned. "I don't know enough about banshees to assist any further."

"So we go to this Sal person ourselves and ask him what he knows. Maybe there's something that he's not telling us?" Ruby said, sitting forwards on the chair. "Taylor is my friend, and I don't have many friends. I won't leave her to fend for herself."

I smiled at the blonde vampire and rested a hand beside her on the chesterfield couch. At this point, I was too afraid to touch any of my friends. Most of them had an aversion to silver, and silver seemed to flow through me.

Ruby rested her cold hand on mine and looked back to her partner. "Will you help us?"

Cole smiled weakly. "Of course, that's not even a question."

I let out a breath that I didn't know I'd been holding. At least if I was facing this fate, I wasn't alone. Again, I had people fighting for me and putting their lives at risk, only this time, *I* was the threat to their lives. Fate can be cruel.

"What about Eden?" Ruby asked. "She managed to keep Taylor in check when she lost control on the last Full Moon."

"Call her, or call Rob, they might know a spell or something." Harper nodded.

"Forgive me, I want to help Taylor, but what is it that we're striving for?" Cole asked. "The grim reaper said that there was no cure. It appears that like vampires, a banshee is clearly an alternative state to true death. To cure her may mean to kill her, and that is not something any of us want."

"I just want control back," I murmured. "I want to not have to worry that with the Full Moon comes the possibility that I hunt and kill one of you."

"It is what Harper faces, is it not?" Cole asked. "But instead of twelve nights a year, he faces thirty-six nights of that."

"Before we worry about any of it, we need to know what we're dealing with… everything that we are dealing with," Harper said, as a curl of maroon smoke appeared beside him.

"You called, I'm here," Eden sighed, looking around at the faces. Her eyes settled on Harper, and she smiled. "Well hello, wolf. I don't believe that we've officially met."

"Eden, I presume." Harper nodded, extending his hand towards her. "I'm Harper Lovett."

"I know," she replied. "I've heard a lot about you from my mum and dad. Sorry it's taken so long for us to meet; I was dealing with a mess that my foster brother got himself into with a Lacer."

"I heard," Harper said. "And the apology is unnecessary."

"So, what's the emergency?" she asked. Everyone looked towards me, and Eden's dark eyes followed. "Who'd she attack this time?"

"Nobody," Ruby replied. "But we now know why she went after me."

"Oh?"

"Taylor is a young banshee," Cole explained. "It is her duty to hunt the supernatural and mark them with death – certain

76

death. After the next Full Moon, she will fully come into her powers."

"Oh, wonderful," Eden breathed. "So what do you want me for? To help arrange a going away party?"

"No one is going anywhere," Harper said slowly. "We asked you here to see if there was any way that you could assist, given your abilities."

"And the way you subdued Taylor on Friday night," Ruby added.

"I don't know how, to be honest." Eden shrugged. "If Taylor was still only coming into her powers as a banshee, then she'll be much stronger when she's a full banshee. I don't really know how strong they get, but if she is as powerful as other Full Moon-driven beings, then the spell won't hold her at all. What else do you know about them? Does silver affect them?"

Ruby shook her head. "No."

"Maybe," I replied.

"But you have silver embedded in your nails." Ruby blinked.

"And yet my nails still scratch me." I shrugged. "Plus, when I picked up silver cutlery the other day, it sort of tingled, and I killed the banshee last time with the silver dagger, remember?"

"That was a hunter's dagger," Cole replied. "It is a little different to other silver."

"How?"

"It's charmed. The silver is melted into shape by a Weaver and cooled by a Lacer. Considering the two aren't normally in agreement on anything, or in the same place for any extended

77

period of time, the magic from the two makes it deadly to anything and everything if struck true, regardless of how silver affects them."

I deflated a little.

"But if you're correct about the cutlery, then maybe your aversion is still present, but just a little more mild than the rest of us given its production within your body," Cole added. "I would say it's that presence that ensures you are not the one to be killed when you hunt."

I shivered at the thought. *When I hunt* because I will hunt. I will go out seeking supernatural to kill.

"One way to find out." Eden shrugged and then vanished in a puff of smoke. A few seconds passed, and she reappeared with a purple bottle and set it in front of me. "Bottoms up, Banshee."

Colloidal silver. Silver particles suspended in water, and my drink of choice the last time I spent so much time around vampires and werewolves. Ironically, it was also used sometimes in alternative medicine to fight off bacteria and other nasties. I hadn't bothered with it much since Harper, and the vampires disappeared from my life, but now it seemed that it was coming back to haunt me. I just wasn't sure whether it would be a help or a hindrance this time around.

"No, Taylor is not drinking that," Harper growled. "If she is affected by silver, then it will poison her."

"And if she isn't, it may strengthen her," Cole said.

Eden rolled her eyes. "So what do you suggest? Stab her with a knife? Testing the theory isn't going to be pleasant either way, and she doesn't have to drink it, just pour some on her and see if her skin bubbles, or whatever happens to you lot."

Everyone exchanged a look, and I exhaled, reaching for the bottle.

"Taylor," Harper breathed. "You don't have to—"

"There's another way," Ruby interrupted.

I stood and headed to the kitchen. It always amused me that there even was a kitchen here, but I suppose that people would find it weird if there was a block of apartments without kitchens. Besides, vampires still needed to wash the blood out of their goblets.

"This is the quickest way," I sighed, unscrewing the lid as I reached the sink. I stretched my arm over the basin and tipped, letting the tinted liquid run over my skin. Again, it felt warm to me, it tingled, but there was no sizzle. I looked over my shoulder at four pairs of eyes staring at me, and then shrugged, lifting the bottle to my lips. I felt it heat my mouth, then burn a path down my throat, bursting out through my body as it reached my stomach. I swayed, resting the purple bottle on the bench before my legs gave way, then coughed weakly as I slipped to the floor.

Harper sprang towards me. "Taylor! Taylor, are you all right?"

I looked up at him and as he stared in my eyes. Worry and something else was painted on his face.

"What?" I murmured. "What's that look?"

"Your eyes," he breathed. "The irises, they… they just flashed white for a second."

"White." I blinked, lifting my hand to touch my face. It didn't quite make it though, because as I raised it, I felt the strength run through it. I stared at my hand and clenched it, feeling every muscle flex. Cole was right. If the silver didn't weaken me, it would strengthen me. It *had* strengthened me. The other day when I touched the silver, it was strength that I felt, not weakness.

I stumbled to stand.

"How do you feel, Taylor?" Cole frowned.

"Fine... great actually." I shrugged. "I think you were right, it had the opposite effect to what it has on you."

"I see."

"So, what now?" Eden shrugged.

"She seems to be virtually indestructible," Cole replied. "The only weakness of ours is the strength of hers. My next line of thinking would be to test our strengths and see how they compare, but all of our strengths differ. To vampires, it lies in venom and blood, to werewolves it comes from the Moon, shifters rely on emotions, and the list goes on."

"What about Weavers?" Eden asked. "What strengthens us?"

"You have a few. Your blood, the red Moon, the elements, emotion."

Eden smiled.

"So, look, the biggest thing now is figuring out if Taylor is a threat to any or all of us, any other time other than a Full Moon at its apex," Ruby said, shaking her head. "The rest of the time could be like normal, then maybe on Full Moon night Taylor just does what Harper does and leaves for the night."

I glanced at Harper then at Ruby.

"You're right," Cole said. "So what do you say we pay a visit to the student housing at SCU?"

The four of us drove in the Jag, in the dying sunlight, towards the university where Sal lived onsite. Eden said she that had somewhere else she needed to be, so disappeared again in her maroon smoke. Cole drove with expert precision, too fast, just like Ruby, but seemed to know the way better than anyone could. Ruby had mentioned once that Cole invested a lot of his time and money in South Coast, and he'd watched the city grow. He had also played a part in designing some of it through his company, *Freeze Frame Architecture and Design*. It wasn't often that I was reminded that Cole was much older than I could comprehend, but when the reminder came, it blew me away.

"It's this way," Cole said, nodding up the road towards where the nursing and philosophy buildings were. I never really thought about where the student housing was, and it surprised me that Cole knew when he wasn't even a student here.

"How come you know where everything is?" I asked, gripping Harper's hand as we made our way up the near-empty street.

"He ought to, he owns it." Ruby smiled. Ruby was wearing a red wig and reading glasses so she wouldn't be recognised by anyone from her human life. She couldn't risk her cover story of moving to Spain for work being blown. Ruby had told me her story once, told me how she had to let go of everything and everyone she knew after becoming a vampire and was forced to hide in plain sight if she wanted to interact with the outside world that was South Coast. It was a small city, but there were still pockets of it where some people never went. Sometimes that was for a good reason.

"You own SCU, Cole?" I gasped. "Is that why Harper transferred so easily? Does that mean that I don't have to keep paying tuition?"

He laughed. "I'll make a call."

Cole led us inside an old building where I had a unit in my first and second year. It smelled old and damp and reminded me of the Amund tomb where I'd spent a couple of days hiding from the wendigo. Just inside the door was a staircase that we all ascended, and at the top, a locked wooden door that led through to a corridor of more doors. He stopped when he reached number seven and waited until Harper, and I caught up.

"This is his room, Taylor, it's a single," Cole murmured. "Perhaps you should be the one to knock."

I nodded and stepped forward, lifting my curled fist and letting it hover over the wooden door before letting it fall against it. There was nothing but silence, then a click, and the door opened. Sal stood in front of us in a pair of black track pants and a black singlet, his orange eyes were framed by black rims, and he held a thick textbook in his arms.

"Well, this is unexpected," he said, removing the pencil from his mouth. He looked passed Harper and I and frowned at the vampires. "Taylor Mistry and her mystical friends."

"Sorry to bother you," I answered.

"Are you?"

"Probably not as much as I should be."

Sal breathed a laugh. "Well, I'd invite you in, but I don't really need to since I don't own this place."

He stepped back, and we all filed into the small room. Cole closed the door behind him.

"I remember you," Sal said pointing at Ruby. "You're the vampire who killed three guys behind *Freeze Frame* a few years ago."

Ruby's silver eyes widened in horror as Sal turned to Cole.

"And you are the vampire who turned her just as I came to reap her after she was hit by the car."

"I see that we need no introduction then," Cole answered. "Let me cut to the chase as to why we're here—"

"Well, whatever it is, I'm not interested. I don't trust vampires," Sal replied, dropping the textbook that he held onto a small coffee table. "I clean up too many humans before their time because of you lot. Not *you* specifically, but the rest of your kind. You, Doctor, have actually saved more lives than taken them the last few years that I've been reaping in South Coast."

"It's not about them," I sighed. "It's about me and my... situation."

Sal folded his arms. "Your situation. You mean you've

83

finally come to terms with the fact that you're a banshee?"

"Well, it's been less than a day; it's a lot to process."

"Sure."

"I just want to know more about what to expect." I shrugged. "I mean, what happens between Full Moons? Will I have control over who I hunt? What happens when I mark someone, or something? And what happens if a human that I know sees me?"

Sal took a breath and let it out.

"You won't hunt your vampire friends if that's any conciliation to you."

"But, Friday night I tried to attack Ruby."

"Really?" He blinked. "Well, maybe that was your human survival instinct kicking in. Vampires are immortal, so banshees rarely touch them. It's more the werewolves and shifters that are your main concern."

"So, I'm going to want to hunt Harper then?" I frowned.

"Not necessarily, not unless it's his time." Sal shrugged. "You'll be able to see it with practice. Their vibe will become clearer to you when their number is up."

"Harper was already hunted by a banshee though. I saved him from it the first time, that's how I got marked."

"But he didn't get marked himself?"

"Well, no," I answered. "But the banshee got her claws into him before I killed it. He nearly died, but the Weavers brought him back."

"From the dead, like?"

"He wasn't dead, he was almost dead."

84

Sal's expression made me nervous.

"What is it?"

"He cheated death," Sal replied. "Fate doesn't normally look kindly on those who cheat death. Everything has a consequence, and yours is that you are now cursed as a banshee."

"Is that how you became a grim reaper?"

Pain flickered across his face. "This isn't about me."

"So can you help her or not?" Harper asked. I turned and noticed that he had pinned himself against the door beside Cole and Ruby, who stood like alabaster statues side by side.

"If Taylor wants, then I can help her adapt to her fate. But no more of this weird vampire-wolf pack stuff," Sal said. "Unlike the rest of you, Taylor and I only exist to make sure that humans don't suffer. We may all need anonymity to continue doing what we do, but we don't need to pretend that we all accept what that is."

I exhaled. "So, that's a yes?"

"As long as you don't bring your pet along, I'll do what I can." He shrugged.

I swallowed back the scathing that moved to the top of my tongue.

"After exams," he added.

I blinked. "Exams?"

"Yes, I'd like to pass my units; they're the week after next. After that, we can start training, or whatever you want to call it."

"But exams go for two weeks," I replied, my voice raising

85

two octaves. "And with this week passing, then study week, by the time they're over, there will be another Full Moon. Isn't that leaving it a little late?"

"No." Sal shrugged. "Your fate is set, you'll make the change. Besides, this one will just bring you into your full capacity. After that is when you'll need guidance. Anything that I say before then won't make a difference. Actually, nothing I say will make a difference. But it helps to know what you're in for, I guess."

My head was shaking, but I exhaled, admitting defeat. "So, what do I do until then?"

"Whatever you normally do. Just be careful with those nails. If there's silver in them, then it means that Full Moon or not, you could still do some damage."

"So, I can't stop it or control it," I breathed. More control lost.

"No, you can't control it," Sal said gravely. "But hey, you said that you know some Weavers. Just make sure you have one of them handy next Full Moon, and I'm sure you'll get through just fine. As for your boyfriend, well I'm sure he already makes himself scarce come Full Moon time of month."

I felt empty, and I wanted to cry, but for some dumb reason, I was too numb to. I looked back at the two vampires and my werewolf boyfriend who still stood like statues against the door.

"Look, I need to study, so if you have no more burning questions, then please feel free to let yourselves out." Sal yawned. "You can leave your number if you want, Taylor

Mistry, I'll be in touch when my exams are done."

The hopelessness that I felt in my heart bubbled into anger, or perhaps it was just me moving onto the second stage of grief due to the loss of my humanity. I hated that I needed Salvatore Vincent's help, I hated that he was so cocky and complacent about my fate—a fate that I didn't even want—and I hated that I couldn't do anything about it. Such is fate. Such is death.

There was nothing left to say, so the four of us went in silence, knowing that nothing we said would make any difference to the hand that had been dealt. As soon as we got back to Cole and Ruby's house, Harper took me home. He kicked the stand of his bike down, then cut the purring engine. Neither of us moved from the bike, but I pulled off my helmet and slipped my free arm around him.

"I'm scared."

His hand brushed my arm. "I know."

"It feels like there's a grenade inside of me, and I know that it's going to go off, but there's nothing that I can do to stop it," I murmured against his back. "How did this happen to me? I'm not human any more, and I didn't even notice. In fact, I felt more different after losing all that weight than I do having been turned into something that's not even human. How dumb is that?"

"It's not dumb, it's… well, I don't know what it is. It's a supernatural circumstance," he replied. I could hear the frown in his voice. "I'm sorry."

"Why are you sorry?"

"If you hadn't saved me that night, you would have never

been marked, you wouldn't have been in danger, or hunted, and you wouldn't be in this mess—"

"Harper, stop," I groaned. "You have to stop. I never ever will regret saving you, ever. So don't even go there. Yes, this sucks, but we're both still alive—"

"For now."

"Well, life is like that, any moment could be our last, so maybe Sal is right. Maybe we should just try and get on with things and accept what we can't change."

Wow, I had jumped right from anger, bypassed bargaining, moved swiftly through depression, and into acceptance. Kübler-Ross would be proud.

I looked up and saw him nod, then waited a moment before finally climbing off the back of his bike.

"Speaking of which." I swallowed. My mouth suddenly felt like sandpaper. "Do you want to stay here tonight?"

Harper looked up, and his brows that were still knitted with worry began to soften. "With you?"

"Well, I wasn't suggesting that you stay with Jesse." I blushed.

He managed a smile. "All right."

"You will?"

"*Oui.*" He nodded, and my heart whipped into a sprint. Harper glanced thoughtfully to the side. "You know, I don't have to stay."

"I want you to stay," I whispered, smacking my hand to my chest. "Don't listen to my heartbeat; it doesn't tell you what my heart feels."

88

Harper nodded and climbed off the black motorbike, sliding his warm hands in mine.

"All right."

Phase Four

The Ghosts of the Past

I could feel Harper's breath on my shoulder, and his steady heartbeat rock the mattress beneath me. His arms were hot and heavy as they pinned me against him. I was not afraid, but I was wide awake.

My eyes were open as the sun greeted the sky, and as the dark hues turned light, my eyelids began to droop. Harper's arms tightened, pulling me against him, and then his breath stopped. I peeked over my shoulder as his light green eyes fluttered open.

"*Bonjour*," he sighed. "I mean, good morning."

I smiled, shuffling around to face him. "Hi."

"You didn't sleep."

"I… what do you mean?"

"You look as if you haven't slept," he noted, his fingers brushing underneath my eyes. "Still beautiful, but a little exhausted."

I pressed my lips together. "A little."

"Did I keep you awake?"

"No," I murmured. "My brain wouldn't switch off. It

seemed to want to solve the world's problems."

The back of his fingers brushed down my cheek. "The world can always wait."

There was scratching on my bedroom door, and I glanced over at it. Raven, my cat. I had locked her out last night because of her aversion to Harper. Apparently, she could sense the wolf-side of him. When he was around, she did nothing but hiss.

"I think your cat misses you." He smirked.

"She can learn to share."

"I don't know if I can."

I felt my cheeks blush and his smile widened. His eyes seemed to glow bright green.

"Cats never really liked you, right?" I sighed. "Well, except for Hunter, I suppose."

The mention of her name sent a strange expression across his face, and his eyes lowered.

"Have you heard from Hunter since she left?" I asked. "Ruby said that she disappeared after everything that happened."

"No, I… no."

"Is it strange that she hasn't been in touch? She mentioned once that you were close, and that meeting you made her stop counting the years," I said, and as I spoke the words, a thought occurred to me. It was one that hadn't even crossed my mind since meeting the stunning Spanish shifter. Being in the same room as her had definitely had lowered my self-esteem, but knowing that Harper relied on her had prickled my jealousy, even before Harper and I had declared our affection for each other. Maybe it was that fleeting, ghostly look on his face that forced those feelings of jealousy to the surface, or perhaps it was my insecurity. Regardless, they were there.

"We… don't always keep tabs on each other," Harper answered slowly. "She… probably needs some time away from me."

"Why?"

"Because it would be hard for her to see me with you," he replied.

"Why?"

"Because before you, there was no one that she needed to share me with."

I pulled back from him and frowned. "Share you? You make it sound as if you were, like, involved."

Harper's brow drew, and I sat up, suddenly feeling very awake.

"Harper, Hunter said that you were as close to her as you get to anyone," I said evenly. "What did she mean by that exactly?"

"It means that we were close," he answered. "We supported each other."

I took a deep breath. "Support how? Like moral support or… other support?"

"What are you asking, Taylor?"

My eyes closed. "Is she a ghost? I mean, did you… did you and her ever…?"

I couldn't even think the words never mind phrase them.

The concept of Harper being intimate with the Mediterranean goddess was too much for my insecurities to handle. I couldn't compare to her, I couldn't compare to her fingernail.

"It's all in the past," he sighed.

I felt as if the air had been sucked out of the room. "So you were… intimate… with her."

He pressed his lips together. "We… for a while. But I never felt for her the way that she did for me."

I climbed out of bed. "Not the point."

"Don't be upset."

"I'm not upset."

"You look upset."

"I… I'm… I don't know what I am," I muttered, opening the door and gasping as the black cat dashed away from fright. Today was not a good day to bring this up, not on no sleep, and not when I was already trying to swallow being a supernatural reaper, and also trying to pass my units for the semester.

"Taylor," Harper sighed, walking after me as I headed to the kitchen.

I stopped when I got there and looked around, not feeling as if food or eating was a good idea. I felt fat and frumpy, I didn't want to eat, not when Hunter could down a bar of chocolate and still look like a runway model. If Harper couldn't fall for *her*, then what hope did I have? I was nowhere near as attractive as her. I lifted my hands to press on my forehead.

"Taylor, stop," Harper murmured, his fingers encircling my wrists. "This is why I didn't want to tell you."

"I feel like a fraud." I pouted.

"A fraud? Why?"

"Because how can you even look at me when she is so much prettier than I am?"

"You are beautiful," he answered.

"Even she said that I wasn't good enough for you," I mumbled, shaking my head. "Maybe she was right."

Harper took my head and rested it against his shoulder, wrapping his arms around me.

"Never," he whispered. "You are too good for me."

"Don't lie."

"I'm not lying."

I frowned, feeling the weight of the lack of sleep on my emotions. "How can I even compete with her?"

"No one is asking you to."

"But I am, regardless," I whimpered, stepping back from him. "You're going to compare me to her whether you mean to or not."

He sighed. "This is crazy, I don't even think of her when I'm with you. All I see is you, Taylor."

I folded my arms and then jumped as another door opened.

"What's going on?" Jesse yawned.

I turned to flick the kettle on to boil. "Sorry, Jess. I didn't know that you were home."

"I got sent home yesterday from work," Jesse murmured sleepily.

"Why?"

"Not sure. I just had this random pain attack midmorning.

It was the same deal last week, but that was at night."

"Are you okay?"

He shrugged. "I feel fine after. It comes and goes, but they still thought that it meant I should rest. Doctors, what do they know?"

I smiled tightly.

"Morning, Harper, you're here early." Jesse nodded. "Or did you not leave last night?"

"I am an adult, Jesse. I can have my boyfriend stay over without asking for permission," I snapped.

Jesse lifted his hands in surrender. "I wasn't implying anything."

"Good."

"What's up with you, Tay?" he asked, his forehead knitting together as his grey eyes looked between Harper and I. "What happened?"

I sighed. "Nothing, don't worry about it."

"No, it's something. You're upset."

"Nothing that you can help with." I muttered. "Nothing that even Harper can help with."

Harper exhaled.

Jesse blinked. "Okay, now I'm really confused."

"I said it's nothing, Jesse, don't worry about me," I groaned. "Leave it alone."

Jesse and Harper exchanged a look that only made me more annoyed. It was stupid, I knew that it was, but it all felt as if I was the punchline of a joke that everyone knew about but me. It never used to bother me, being inexperienced with boys,

I never let it affect me because I had other things to occupy my time. But now, now it felt as if I was miles behind everyone, and that I had missed some initiation into a secret club for members only. I felt like a kid trying to keep up with adult conversation, or that person who gets sympathy for not being picked on anyone's team. What's more, I heard Eden's stupid taunting voice in my head, and it made me want to scream.

"Harper, can I get you a coffee or something?" Jesse yawned. "Since my lovely sister is clearly having a breakdown."

Harper frowned. "Do you have espresso?"

"Only the best."

Harper sighed. "Better make it a double."

*

"Was it just Hunter? How long did your little affair go on for?" I asked as we walked into uni from where Harper's bike was parked. Two hours had passed, and I had been pretty quiet since snapping unnecessarily at Jesse. I had gone about making my own breakfast as the two boys spoke candidly like old friends. They both seemed to watch me with the same concern that one might watch a boiling pot on the stove – like they were waiting for the bubbles to erupt out the top.

"Taylor, stop," Harper sighed. "Don't do this."

"I want to know."

His head shook. "No, you don't. You think that you do, but you don't."

"How many other girls aside from Hunter were there?"

"Taylor…"

I planted my feet. "Do you think that I'll get mad because there are heaps?"

"There are not that many," he said. "And you have no reason to get mad at me because of my past relationships, just as I would never get mad at you for yours."

"Mine? I have none!" I squeaked. "That's my point!"

His eyebrow lifted. "None? I do believe that when I met you that your affections were elsewhere – divided even?"

My mouth popped open. "Leo and I were… and Brandon… no!"

He shrugged. "As I said, it is none of my concern."

"And even after you… you told me to move on; you wanted me to see other guys because you said that you weren't boyfriend material."

"I know."

"So, don't get all judge-y on me." I frowned.

"Like I said," he murmured, resting his hands on my shoulders. "None of that is a concern to me. All that concerns me is here and now, you and me, and nothing else matters."

My mouth opened and Harper's finger nudged my chin to close it. "No. No more."

"Just give me a number."

"No."

"Please?"

He shook his head. "No."

"I'll keep asking."

"I'll keep saying no."

97

"You're driving me crazy." I pouted.

"Well, clearly we're headed in the same direction." He smirked.

I smiled despite myself. "I'm insecure."

"I noticed."

"I'm sorry," I breathed. "I know that you love me."

He nodded. "I do."

"But I don't understand why you wouldn't love Hunter." I shrugged. "She's flawless."

"She's not you."

I mashed my lips together. "I guess she's not as nice as I am."

He laughed. "No, she's not."

I smiled. "Okay."

"Okay?"

"I'll drop it." I nodded.

"*Magnifique,*" he sighed. "Now let me walk you to class."

I couldn't concentrate in class either, and I couldn't decide whether it was the lack of sleep, the reason for the silver growing in my nails, or the completely unreasonable thoughts about Harper and his romantic history with his feline friend. It shouldn't bother me. I knew that there had to have been girls with before me. But Harper was right, knowing anything about the ghosts was so much worse. I just couldn't understand what made me better suited for Harper than Hunter was. She knew what it meant to have control, she knew about the world that he had been thrown into at four years old, she wasn't caught up with *first world problems* like my struggle with food. I didn't want to compete with ghosts, but now I felt like I was competing with real people. The stupid thing was that it wasn't even a competition, because Harper had chosen me. He loved *me*.

Regardless, I couldn't help but run over the conversation that I'd had with Hunter from when she'd been instructed to look after me at her house – the house that Harper now occupied. My heart sank further. *"Do not bother falling for him,"* she told me. *"Whatever he may feel for you will not last; it never does. He's different to the boys you are used to. Do not get too attached."*

Somewhere inside me, I knew that the words didn't apply to me because I had broached that barrier that cut him off from the others…

"…Which will also be in your final exam," my lecturer said. I snapped back into reality and looked up. Crap, what would be in the exam? "That's all for today and for the semester. Good luck everyone."

I groaned internally. Perfect, what a completely costly waste of time. My semester hadn't been the easiest first one back, and I apparently was ensuring that I wouldn't pass it. At least Sal had his priorities straight. Ugh, Sal – the reaper, because I needed him to teach me how to be one for the supernatural.

And to think my biggest concern used to be food.

Hunter was right; it really was a first world problem.

Ugh, Hunter.

"How was class?" Harper smiled.

I sighed. "I really need to study."

"I think that is a good use of time."

I went onto my other classes and then met Harper again at

lunchtime at the esplanade. Neither of us liked the common room much, and the park was where we'd had our first real conversation. When we were there, it felt like we were in our place.

*

The rest of the week followed much the same as my units wound down, and I tried to put everything else out of my head. The things I couldn't control. Study was something that I could control. This fate was up to me. So, why was my brain hell-bent on focusing on the other stuff? Was it a part of being human to worry, and to want to try and fix everything, even when there was no means to? But was I even human any more?

"Hey," a voice murmured on Sunday morning. I was cowering over my notebook at the kitchen table. I looked up and smiled tentatively at Ashley.

"Hi."

"Exams?"

I nodded.

"Can I make you breakfast or have you already eaten?" she asked.

I blinked. "Um, I've eaten… already… thanks."

"Sorry," she sighed. "I won't distract you."

I shook my head. "You're not. I should probably take a break anyway. I've been studying since sunrise."

She yawned. "That's dedication."

"I need to be dedicated. I've been really distracted lately, so

I'm a bit behind. I can't afford to fail any units because, after taking that year off, I set myself back. I still have a year and a half to go after this one, and that's long enough."

Ashley nodded, and I wondered if I'd just bored her into silence.

"Sorry," I sighed. "You probably don't care."

"Of course I care," she answered. "I don't know why you have this idea about me that I... I'm the big bad wolf or something."

I laughed slightly hysterically. "I don't think that."

"I'm not as dumb as you think, Taylor, I know that you've never liked me that much, and maybe I haven't made it easy for you, but you are rather intimidating." She shrugged.

"Me? Intimidating?" I frowned.

Her eyebrows rose. "You and Jesse are twins, so I know that makes you quite close. When Jesse and I first got together, I never intended to come between the two of you, but I know that I did. I know that because of it, you resented me even from before you got to know me."

I folded my arms defensively because they were my only shield. "I guess you're sort of right about that."

"All I've ever wanted was to be your friend, or at least someone who you don't hate for loving your brother."

"I don't hate you, Ashley," I murmured. "I'll admit that I never particularly liked you because I felt like you were stealing Jesse from me. But I didn't hate you, and I don't think that you're dumb. Jesse wouldn't date a dumb girl."

She breathed a laugh. "There's a compliment in there

somewhere, I'm sure."

"Why didn't you ever say anything?" I asked. "I mean, you and Jesse have been together for, like, two years, and you're telling me that all that time you were intimidated by me?"

"Well, you can be quite dismissive."

I made a face.

"Do you remember when we first met?" she said, sliding into the chair beside me. "Jesse invited me over for dinner with you and your parents, and you didn't speak directly to me until halfway through the night."

I frowned at the memory. Sure, I remembered it. I remembered it well. It was before I went to Europe and changed my life before I had any amount of confidence in myself at all, and when I felt like food was something that was killing me rather than fuelling me. I hated formal dinners. I hated eating in front of people because I felt as if there was a spotlight on the overweight girl. No one ever said anything, but I felt judged by their gaze if I ever reached for seconds.

"I… I remember that." I nodded. "I remember Jesse ripping into me after you left because he thought that I was rude to you. I remember resenting you more for it. I didn't like to talk about it then, but it really wasn't you, I promise. I wasn't in a good place with myself and, as a result, I punished away everyone around me, especially those who didn't have to try so hard to be happy with themselves."

I wiped the moisture away from under my eyes, a side effect of the stroll down memory lane and a few sleepless nights. The ghosts of the past were never easy to confront.

102

"I didn't know that Jesse got mad at you because of that night," she whispered. "But I know that afterwards, talking to you felt more like you were filling a pleasantry quota rather than anything else."

I pressed my lips together in a tight smile. "I guess it felt like I was."

"Look, I know that a lot of time has passed, and both of us are to blame for not trying to understand where the other is coming from," she murmured. "But I love Jesse a lot, and I hope to be with him for a long time. So maybe we can at least try to work on getting to know each other a little better, and then maybe one day we can be friends?"

"Okay." I nodded. "That sounds fair."

She smiled, and her brown eyes looked warmer than I'd ever seen them when they looked at me.

"You know, when Jesse first told me that he had a twin sister, I was so jealous," she sighed. "I only have an older brother, and he's a lot older, so I don't see him much. He moved out when I was about ten."

I shook my head. "I didn't know that."

She nodded. "Jesse used to tell me a lot about you before I got to meet you, and the way he spoke about you, I felt like I already knew you, and we were already friends, or sisters, I don't know. He built you up so much that I was scared to meet you, just in case you didn't like me and he couldn't be with someone who didn't get along with his... his soul mate. Because you are, you two are soul mates."

Tears flooded my vision again.

103

"I'm really sorry, Ashley."

She shook her head. "I'm not telling you this to make you feel bad, I'm telling you this, so you understand where I'm coming from as an outsider. I never had a close relationship with my brother, so I don't understand it. But I do appreciate it. Like I said, I never wanted to come between that, I wanted to try and be a part of it, but it was naïve to think that I could just step in and be welcomed with open arms."

"It should have been like that," I whispered. "My parents were like that."

"It's different between you two though, I get it." She nodded, and I could see the tears in her eyes too. "You felt like you were losing a brother when I felt like I was gaining a sister."

I took off my reading glasses and rubbed my wet eyelashes. "I never thought of it like that."

"I'm sorry for making you cry." She laughed through her own tears. "This is far too deep for a Sunday morning."

I laughed. "And here I was studying Animal Systems and Veterinary Professional Life."

She reached out and patted my hand, and I turned my palm over to grasp hers.

"Let's be friends, okay?" I said. "We're adults, we can do this."

She grinned. "I'd really like that."

I heard Jesse's yawn before I saw his mass of ash-blond hair appear. He blinked at Ashley and me, and then rubbed his eyes.

"Am I dreaming or am I dead?" he mumbled. "Because you two look like you're talking to each other *and* smiling at the same time, so I *know* this can't be based in reality."

"Sure it can." I shrugged. "Stranger things have happened, trust me."

Jesse pulled a face as he stepped between us, resting a hand on each of our shoulders.

"Oh yeah? What things?"

"Things you probably wouldn't believe anyway." I yawned.

"Mm-hm." He nodded, backing towards the kitchen. "So where's Harper this morning?"

"His place."

"Did you guys make up yet?"

I blinked. "We were never fighting."

Jesse made a noise of amusement. "So, what was with your little spat on Tuesday then?"

"It wasn't a spat," I groaned. "He... he just didn't mention something that sort of made me a little paranoid."

Jesse returned to the table with a glass of orange juice. "What about?"

"Darling, leave it alone," Ashley said. "Taylor might not want to talk about it right now."

I smiled at her. "It was about someone he used to be with, I guess. She's just sort of perfect, and I feel like inadequate compared to her."

"But he's not with her any more." Jesse shrugged. "He's with you."

"Thank you, Captain Obvious."

"Doctor. It's Doctor Obvious."

I rolled my eyes. "I know that he's with me, but what can I offer him that she couldn't? Like, if he couldn't love her and stay with her, then what hope do I have?"

"I think that you're over thinking it, sis," Jesse replied, taking a sip. I glanced at Ashley.

"Do you think I'm being silly?"

She looked a little surprised to be asked. "No, I think you're being human. It's natural to compare yourself to other people, but I think that, at the end of the day, you have to remember that he is with you, and if he wanted her then he wouldn't have ended things with her in the first place. You can't be anyone but yourself, and he knows who you are, and he likes that. He loves that. Anyone can see that the guy is smitten with you."

I nodded and felt a smile tug at the corner of my lips. "I guess so."

"I know so," Ashley replied.

"Yup, I'm dreaming." Jesse huffed. "Or dead, this is my afterlife where finally my sister and my girlfriend aren't fighting like cats and dogs."

Ashley smirked. "Who are you calling a dog?"

I tipped my head. "They're not as bad as you think."

The two of them looked at me and smiled. For a moment, I thought that maybe I was dreaming too... or dead. Stranger things have happened.

*

Sunday afternoon I had planned to go to Ruby and Cole's place to catch up with Ruby, considering I hadn't seen much of her since the Monday night when Sal sealed my fate. I was a bit nervous about going back to see the vampires knowing what I was now, but at least I also knew that as a banshee, I wouldn't be going after any of the immortals.

I made my way up to their penthouse apartment, scanning my palm print in the elevator, and waited until I reached the top. When the steel doors opened to the floor, I could hear voices. It was unusual that they were so loud, considering most supernaturals had great hearing, so the need for volume was moot. As I got closer, I heard a familiar Spanish accent and felt ice run down my spine.

"What do you mean it's not safe?" the voice was saying. "If it is not safe for me, it is not safe for Harper, then we both should leave."

I froze. *Leave? Both?*

"Hunter, I already told you that I am not leaving Taylor," Harper replied. Harper was here too?

"What is it with you and that insignificant girl?" Hunter hissed. "Has she not done enough? You need her to kill one of us too?"

"Do not speak about her that way," Harper roared. "Or do I need to remind you how this conversation ends?"

"Please." Hunter scoffed. "Spare me the details of this supposed *love* you have for the girl. I never took you for a masochist, Lovett, but you are really making a good impression of one."

"Shh, she's here," Ruby's low voice murmured. There was a pause, and I cursed my rapidly beating heart and their impeccable hearing.

"Taylor?" Harper asked, stepping into view. He smiled weakly. "Hi."

I nodded. "Hi."

"Hunter is here. She's back."

"I heard."

Ruby's friendly pale face appeared. "Are you going to come in?"

I wasn't sure myself, but I didn't need to be, because Harper came out and took my hand, towing me into where the four other figures stood. Four, not three as I'd expected. The fourth was someone who I hadn't seen before. He had light brown, almost sandy-coloured hair that was overgrown around his ears, and curious brown eyes. He hung back from the others, my friends, but stood behind Hunter, which led me to believe that he was familiar with her.

"Hunter." I nodded.

"Human," she sighed. Her Spanish accent still making the words directed at me sound more hostile than necessary. "Or is it *banshee* now? Since I hear that, come the Full Moon, you are going to be the one hunting us from now on."

So that was what this was about. Hunter's protective impulses of Harper were in full swing. Whisk him away before the dangerous girl fulfils her fate and is everyone's demise.

"Um, not if I can help it," I answered.

"Well, as it turns out, you can't."

I sighed. "You're right. I can't help it, I can't control my changing any more than you can control yours, so back off. I didn't choose to become this, but I became it because that was the cost of saving Harper's life. It's a cost that I would pay again in a heartbeat. *You* are not the only one who would risk your life for him."

Hunter fumed as Harper's lips twitched and his hand tightened in mine. I noticed another shift from the corner of my eye as the new addition shuffled his weight.

"Who's that?" I whispered to Harper. It was pointless whispering unless the addition was a human one, though something told me that he wasn't.

"*That* is André," Hunter hissed, answering my question despite it not being directed at her. "We met in Canada."

My head tipped. "Is that where you were all this time?"

"Did I stutter?"

A growl rumbled in Harper's chest.

"Hi, I'm Taylor," I said to André. "I'm sure you've heard a lot about me, that only some of which is true."

Hunter scoffed, and André stepped forward.

"Hello, Taylor," he said, smiling a little.

I blinked at his accent. "You don't sound Canadian."

"I am French-Canadian."

My eyebrows lifted. I guess Hunter had a type.

Harper huffed. "That is not real French."

André said something quick and low that I didn't catch. It was too fast for my beginner's French to pick up.

Harper shook his head. "*Non.*"

I heard a chuckle and looked over to see Cole. The vampires were so quiet that I'd almost forgotten they were here.

"So, are you a shifter too, like Hunter?" I asked André before an argument over languages broke out.

"*Oui.*" He nodded, glancing at Harper who rolled his eyes. "Although, unlike Hunter, I am not a beautiful black jaguar, I shift into a cougar."

"I read that there's a large population of those in western Canada."

"*Oui*, but I am from Quebec, which is eastern Canada."

Hunter lifted her hands. "Enough of the chatter, it is boring me."

I rolled my eyes.

"Look, Harper, when you called, I thought that by coming here I could help you see reason, but clearly this girl still has you blinded—"

"I did not call you for—"

"As I said last time," Hunter continued. "I will not sit idly by and watch you participate in a suicide mission over this girl."

Harper exhaled. "I did not ask you to come—"

"Regardless," she sighed. "I am here, and I am not leaving without you."

Harper straightened. "And I am not leaving Taylor."

Hunter began stringing a lot of harsh-sounding Spanish words together that made Cole's eyes widen.

"It is *never* going to end well with her, Lovett, can't you see?" she screeched. "One of you will die for the sake of this ridiculousness, and given it is now *her* who holds more power, I will not let it be *you*."

"You do not get a say in this," Harper growled, releasing my hand as he stepped forward. I took a step back and felt exceedingly awkward as if I was witnessing some kind of weird-pseudo breakup. Something twisted in my stomach when I realised it probably was something like that. Hunter never wanted to let go.

"I did not ask you to come here, I called to make sure that you were still *alive* because *no one* had heard so much as a *purr* from you in months," Harper said angrily. "Do not mistake my concern for something else!"

Hunter's face went red, and then black – very black and furry as she burst out of her skin and into the form of the black panther that had once fought in my defence. The large cat roared and snapped at me, pacing around the small formation that we had made. Instinctively, Harper's body moved in front of mine, but it was not my safety that was concerning to me. My hands gripped his.

"Enough!" Cole exclaimed, walking between them like some kind of animal tamer. "This is clearly getting us nowhere. Harper, Taylor, my apologies, but perhaps you should both go and give Hunter a chance to pull herself together."

I glanced over at Ruby who smiled apologetically, then back at the black jaguar, which was now being stroked by André.

Harper took a calming breath and nodded.

"I am truly sorry for the scene that we have caused. It was

111

most impolite and completely unacceptable behaviour."

"Apologies accepted, my friend," Cole replied. "We are all a little on edge right now."

Harper lowered his head in another nod and turned to farewell Ruby before leading me back towards the elevator. Neither of us spoke as we made our way down to the basement, but I could see the swirl of emotions in his eyes – sadness, anger, regret, worry. I wished that there was something that I could do to replace them with the happiness that usually made them glow.

The doors opened into the dark area, and we stepped out. Harper led me over to my four-wheel drive and stopped by the driver's door.

"I am sorry that I ruined your afternoon with Ruby," he whispered, lowering his head. "I did not know that Hunter was in South Coast until an hour ago when Cole called me and said that she was at the apartment."

My hands moved to cradle his face. "It's not your fault, don't worry about it."

"It is my fault. I called her. She is here because of me."

I frowned, knowing that I couldn't deny that much. She *was* here because of him, and because she didn't want to see him harmed by me.

"What?" Harper breathed. "What's wrong?"

"She's just worried about you." I couldn't believe that the words had come out of my mouth.

"She doesn't need to be."

"She does." I shrugged. "I could mark you. That is a

112

reality."

His head shook in my hands. "I trust you."

"It's not about trust. I don't get to pick. Fate does."

"I trust fate too," he said. "Our fate, the fate where you and I are together, and nothing supernatural or otherwise stands in the way."

I bit my lip. "It might not be that simple."

His hands rested on my wrists. "Do not tell me that you have doubts now."

"Not about you. I am concerned that I'll hurt you though, or worse."

"Once a month – the Full Moon. That's the only time that you are a danger to me. Just like the way I was to you. Nothing has changed between us except for the fact that we are on a level playing field, and now you can protect yourself."

"And I can hurt you," I murmured. "I can't deal with the fact that I am capable of that now."

His head shook. "Don't do that. Don't say that when ten weeks ago I was millimetres away from killing you, and even then you would not hurt me to save yourself. If that is not blind faith then what is?"

I looked into his olive-green eyes as they pleaded with me.

"I love you, Taylor," he whispered. "So I will not allow this to defeat us. If anything, it will make what we have stronger – better than normal, paranormal."

I smiled weakly as his forehead rested against mine.

"I love you, Taylor, so I have faith that this won't be the end of our story, it's merely a twist in the road."

My arms moved to encircle his neck, and I rose to my toes to hug him.

"I love you too, to the Moon and back."

He sighed. "*À la lune et retour.* Always."

Phase Five

The First Reap

I spent a lot of time on campus during study week to make the most out of the library and laboratory. Harper stayed close by, but considering he was doing his Masters in Molecular Biology, he had to focus more on writing his thesis than anything else. My exams were mostly in the first week, with only one in the second, so at least by the time the Full Moon came, my semester would be over.

Hunter returned to live at the park-side house, which meant that Harper was spending more time at my house and in my bed. It took me two nights of being wide awake before I got tired enough to not worry about the fact that Harper was beside me, and his arms were around me. Two nights of worrying that I wanted more from him, but not knowing if I could give it to him. Doubting myself, always doubting myself.

"There's no Moon tonight," Harper whispered on Friday night as he tucked my hair behind my shoulder. We were lying in my bed, but it was still relatively early in the evening. "It's the safest night of the month for us both."

"Safe."

"Do you not feel safe?" he asked. "Your heart is beating really fast."

"That's because of you, not because I feel unsafe."

He smiled. "Me?"

"Yes, you still have the ability to make me nervous," I said, feeling myself blush.

"Why?"

I played with the ends of my hair. "Because I want to be close to you, but I don't know how."

He shuffled towards me, and I swallowed, feeling his hand run down my arm.

"Like this?" he whispered, sinking his lips onto mine. I exhaled into the kiss and felt my toes tingle. I could hear my heartbeat in my ears, and the sound was so loud that you didn't need supernatural hearing to hear it. My lungs felt tight as I crushed myself against Harper's frame. My breathing came out in short, embarrassing bursts.

"Harper," I sighed.

"Mm?"

"I don't…"

"You're doing just fine," he exhaled, gripping my hand and lifting to pin it beside my head. His lips trailed down my chin, dipping below my neck as his finger brushed down my arm, sliding under the neckline of my singlet as they continued down to my waist. I was too absorbed to feel self-conscious, too flustered to be embarrassed that his hands were the first to touch me and set off electrical impulses beneath my skin. My hands trembled as my fingers skimmed his sides, gripping the fabric of his cotton T-shirt to try to push it up his insanely toned body. Realising what I was doing he pulled back, tugging his shirt off in one smooth movement and tossed it aside. My heart felt like it was going to erupt.

"Are you okay?" he whispered.

I gulped and nodded, lifting my hand to trace the freckles on his shoulder and chest.

He smiled and lay back down beside me. "Too close?"

"No."

"Still nervous?"

I bit my lip. "You always make me nervous. Just the way you look at me makes my heart race."

"I like that I have that effect on you, but I don't want you to be nervous. I told you, whatever you're comfortable with."

My hand climbed his collarbone and settled on his neck. "I am comfortable with you. It's just that sometimes I'm not comfortable with myself."

He leant in to kiss me, and I sighed. Gosh, this guy would be my demise, but considering what else I had faced, I was somehow okay with that.

*

"Morning, Taylor." Brandon nodded on Monday morning over his bowl of cereal.

"Hi."

"Exam this morning?"

"Afternoon," I replied. "You?"

117

"Tomorrow." He shrugged. "Harper didn't stay last night?"

I frowned. "No, he… no."

"No trouble in paradise, I hope."

"No, we're stronger than ever actually," I answered. "How's Amelia Saber going?"

He made a face. "We're not together any more. Turns out she was interested in someone else."

"Oh," I said. "Sorry to hear."

"Sure you are."

I sighed and headed to the kitchen to make some oat bran porridge.

"Actually, I'm seeing someone else now," he continued. "I think she said she knows you."

My hand froze mid-tablespoon scoop, and I frowned. "Who would I know that would actually date you?"

Brandon chuckled. "Very funny. Her name is Eden."

Oh, crap. "Eden? I hope you're kidding."

"Why? Jealous?"

I peered out at him from behind the wall. "No, but she'll *crush* you."

"I'm up for the challenge." He grinned. I wondered if he knew that she could literally poison him with a kiss, or send electricity through his cells, or set his scruffy blond hair on fire.

"How did you even meet her?"

"She was on campus because of some fire in the dorms near the gym," he said with a shrug. "She's a firefighter. How hot is that?"

I wasn't really surprised, I guess. Eden's father Rob was a

firefighter, and given that Weavers manipulate fire and could heal themselves, it was probably the most perfect occupation for them – that and an electrician, since electricity was another one of their strengths.

"Oh." I nodded belatedly. "Wait. Did you say fire in the dorms? Like the student housing on campus?"

"Yup, last week. Didn't you hear?"

"Obviously not." I frowned. "So what happened to the people living in them? Are they still there? How bad was the damage?"

Brandon pulled a face. "Taylor, how would I know this?"

"Well, you know something about it. What did Eden say?"

"We don't talk much, to be honest."

I rolled my eyes, left the porridge, and grabbed my keys. "I'm heading into uni, see you later."

"You're skipping breakfast?" Brandon called. "You?"

"They do have food outside of my kitchen."

He huffed. "Do they?"

I scooped my bag and closed the door, hurrying towards my car. If there was a fire in student housing, where was Sal? Why hadn't Cole or Ruby mentioned anything? Did they know? Eden was there, so surely she must have said something. I hit dial on the way and linked up my hands-free.

"Taylor? Is everything okay?" Ruby asked.

"Hey, Ruby, I'm fine. I… did you know that there was a fire in student housing at SCU last week?" I replied. "Apparently Eden was there."

"A fire? No."

119

I sighed. "I'm heading in there now, but I'm guessing if you or Cole don't know about it then it can't have been that bad."

"*Cole is more of a benefactor, so not necessarily,*" she answered. "*But given it wasn't publicised, I would say that it was only superficial damage.*"

I exhaled. "I just hope Sal is all right, he still needs to help me with this, um, stuff."

"*I'm sure that he's fine, he's probably protected as a grim, but let me know what you find out.*"

I nodded then realised that I was on the phone. "I will, thanks, Rubes."

"*Later, Tay.*"

My eyes lowered to hang up, and then I gasped, slamming on my brakes as the car in front stopped at a red light. Maybe now that I was a baby banshee, I was a little more durable than I used to be, but that didn't mean I wanted to test that theory, or kill any humans in the process. I made an effort to concentrate on the rest of the short drive to campus as to not give Sal any more work in reaping. Apparently, my friends had given him enough.

I headed straight to his dorm, nearly face-planting up the stairs as I ran. Once upon a time, not so long ago, running was my forte. I suppose I'd slacked off a little since the exercise had saved my life.

My fist collided with his door as I caught my breath. After a painful pause, it opened.

Sal sighed. "Taylor Mistry."

"Sal," I breathed. "Salvatore Vincent."

"To what… are you doing here?" he asked. "On a Monday morning, during exams, panting like a *wolf*."

I straightened. "I was worried. I heard about the fire."

"Fire," he repeated. "From last week? You're a little behind the eight-ball, Mistry."

"I know."

His head tipped. "Were you worried about me?"

"Don't read into it." I shrugged. "I just don't want you disappearing before I get my answers."

"Ah, yes, well I'm no expert, but I know a little. Do you want to come inside? Considering the topic of conversation is a little… delicate?"

I scratched my eyebrow and stepped in. Sal closed the door behind me and pulled off his singlet, I turned back towards the door.

"Relax, I'm finding another shirt." He chuckled. "You caught me still in my pyjamas."

I frowned. "As long as the pants stay on."

"You're a little squeamish, aren't you, Taylor Mistry?"

"I have a boyfriend."

"Does he keep his pants on too?"

"His pants aren't any of your concern."

Sal laughed. "Okay."

"So what did you want to talk to me about that is delicate?" I asked. "Not your pants, I hope."

His eyebrows lifted and fell. "No, actually. I was saying that I'm no expert on your side of death – the supernatural reaping and such. But I have been trying to get in touch with Alba to see if she could shed any light for you."

"Who is Alba?"

"The banshee that I knew, the one that I haven't seen in a while," he replied, pulling a black T-shirt over his head.

I nodded. "Oh, and?"

He shook his head. "Vanished without a trace. South Coast was her area, so I'm guessing that it was her that you killed and replaced."

"Her area?" I blinked. "There are areas? I don't understand."

"Well it's no good all the reapers chilling in the one place, there needs to be a balance so balance can be kept," he answered. "They're not like hunters, those guys cluster more in certain locations that are higher in supernatural numbers."

Hunters like Leo, my Italian flame that ended up trying to kill Harper. It was a little scarring to discover that the elaborate romance between us was just so he could get to Harper. The question of whether it started out that way constantly played on my mind, but the answer was that it certainly ended whatever was between us because of it.

"So, why do hunters exist if banshees exist?" I asked. "Don't they sort of do the same thing?"

Sal shook his head. "Banshees keep order, hunters reject the unexplainable."

"A bit like philosophers then?"

"More like scientists actually." He smirked. "Philosophers strive for knowledge, scientists strive for answers. Not all things fit into the black or the white, sometimes they're grey – or silver, as it were."

"So, how do you fit into it?" I shrugged. "I take it you were a regular human once? How are grims made?"

"We're reapers," he corrected. "People perceive death as being grim, so they add that to the title, but essentially we just reap. Death isn't always pretty, but it doesn't have to be ugly and uninviting."

"Okay." I nodded. "So how did you become a *reaper*?"

Sal frowned, looking as if he wasn't going to tell me. I'd hit this wall before, and he'd changed the subject.

"I was a regular human once, but I don't really remember it," he answered. "I was seven."

"You were seven?" I blinked. Harper had told me that he was four when he became a wolf, but dealing with death. Witnessing it repeatedly at such a young age seemed far crueler fate.

"Yes, seven," he said. "My family were all killed in a house fire, and the reaper who took them had mercy on me. So, here I am guiding souls into the afterlife."

"Some fate."

"It's your fate too," he noted. "Only yours is a little worse. You're a human kissed by the supernatural, and now you not only take their souls, but you also have to hunt their lives."

I shivered. "I won't do that."

"You don't get the choice, Taylor. Instinct will take over."

I shook my head. "You mentioned that werewolves and shifters were my main concern, what about Weavers?"

"What about Weavers?" he asked. "Weavers and Lacers are

tricky because they're still human in many ways, but I guess so are werewolves. But Weavers tend to use magic against banshees to evade them, same goes for Lacers, but they're already a dying breed. Basically, if they have any kind of supernatural or superhuman quality to them, it's on you."

"Including reapers?"

He smiled. "Taylor Mistry, you wouldn't."

I laughed, and Sal suddenly cringed. His eyes closed and then his forehead puckered.

I frowned. "Are you okay?"

"I need to go," he breathed. "Duty calls."

"Exams?"

"Other duty."

"Reaper duty?"

He nodded. "Do you, um, do you want to come?"

"Can I come?"

He shrugged. "I haven't tried it before, but if you keep hold of my hand, you should stay invisible to people. The only catch is that you will feel what I'm feeling, and what they feel."

I swallowed. "Is that the same thing that a banshee experiences?"

"I don't know, to be honest."

I bit my lip. "Okay. Where are we going?"

He reached out and took my hand, and I felt myself being sucked away from my current surroundings and pop out in a white hospital room. I forced a yawn to ease the compression in my ears and then looked around.

"Oh my gosh, it's my dad," I whispered.

Sal looked at me. "The patient?"

"No, the doctor."

"Oh, sure, Doctor Mistry." He nodded. "I see Jack quite a bit. I guess I should have put that one together. It is South Coast, after all. Everyone seems to be related here."

I pressed my lips together and Sal tipped his head towards the dying old man, the rhythmic beeps beside him swallowed out by the raspy breaths that he struggled to take.

"Stay quiet now, because when I touch him, he'll be able to see us," he whispered. "Leave the talking to me, okay?"

I gave a curt nod and let him tug me forward towards the bed. As soon as Sal's hand made contact with the dying man, I felt everything that he was feeling, and my insides twisted with pain.

"You're not alone," Sal murmured. I looked at him, wondering if he was talking to me, but saw his eyes were focused on the man. "You're safe. Everything is going to be okay. You can let go. Everything is okay, you're free."

The man's weary eyes opened, and he tried to smile. His throat protested as he tried to take one last breath that seemed to be lodged sideways in his windpipe. Sal's grip tightened, and the pain passing through me got more intense as the man exhaled and the life support let out one elongated *beep*.

It took everything that I had not to scream or show the amount of agony squeezing within me, suffocating me like nothing I'd never felt before – not drowning when I was six, not running for my life, or even when the banshee crushed down on me. Nothing compared to this. It was grim and dark, and hollow. It was death.

Sal exhaled in a huff, as if he'd also been holding his breath, and then stumbled back from the bed. His orange eyes glanced over at me then I felt myself being pulled back, and suddenly, we were standing back in his dorm room. Both of us stood in silence for a long time, not moving, barely breathing, and not releasing our hold of each other.

Then I burst into tears.

"Hey, are you okay?" Sal breathed. "I'm sorry. I guess I'm used to it now."

"That was horrible," I cried, sinking to my knees. "Is it always like that? That... that intense? That painful?"

"Always. Though they usually take much longer than that," Sal murmured solemnly, crouching beside me to rest his hand on my shoulder. "I'm sorry if it hurt you."

"You're sorry? You've had to experience that on a daily basis from when you were just a kid."

"More than daily, people die all the time. At least I'm not the only reaper around."

I whimpered. "Oh gosh, Sal. How do you do it?"

"It's not about me. I take away *their* suffering, and I allow *them* to rest in peace," he replied. "It's a big responsibility, so I don't take it lightly. It's just my job."

I brushed the wetness from my cheek. "You're amazing."

He drew in a breath and let it out. "Yeah, I know."

I rolled my eyes.

"Are you hungry?" he asked. "Have you eaten breakfast? Because I haven't, and I'm famished."

"No, I haven't actually. I sort of left home in a hurry."

"To check on me, right?" He smirked, rising to his feet and offering me his hand. "Come on, I'll shout you."

I slapped my hand in his and pulled myself up to stand. "*Shout me?* Cute."

"Cute, amazing, wise, attractive – how you flatter me, Miss Mistry."

"You're also ridiculous, Sal."

He chuckled. "So, do you have a preference of location? There are a few places close like *Excalibur* and whatever, but I know this little French café called—"

"*Clair de Lune?*" I asked. "I know it."

"Of course, I bet the wolf took you there, being somewhat French and a bit of a lunatic himself," he said. "Clair de Lune means *moonlight* in French, right?"

I blinked slowly. "Lunatic? He's not a psychopath, he's a werewolf."

"He loses control depending on the lunar cycle, he's a lunatic."

I shook my head. "Why do you do that? Just stop with the quips and jibes, it's unnecessary."

"Sorry." He huffed. "I guess it's a defence mechanism. Plus, I guess you're sort of one too now, right? A slave of the Moon."

I frowned. "I guess so."

Sal pressed his lips together. "Why don't we just go to *Excalibur?*"

"Okay."

*

I could still feel the ghost of the dying man's pain pulse through me as I sat in my three-hour exam that afternoon. As much as I willed myself to forget it, even for a while, it resonated in my cells, my pores, and in the pit of my stomach. The death, my first reap, the pain. What would it be like to be responsible for that? Come the Full Moon, I would not only be responsible, but I would have to *hunt* for my victims. *I* would decide that someone's clock has run out. The thought plagued me as much as the reminder of the pain. I couldn't focus, and it frightened me.

By the time 'pens down' was called, I had barely finished what was in front of me, but I felt mentally drained of information. I could have done better, I *should* have done better, and now the fate of my future was under a cloud of doubt.

"How did you go?" Harper smiled as I stepped out the drill hall.

"Not great."

"No, Taylor, why?"

I pouted. "I… something happened this morning, and I can't stop thinking about it… and about next Saturday night."

I didn't have to explain to Harper what next Saturday was – being a werewolf, he kept track of the Full Moon cycles already.

"What happened?" he asked.

I shook my head, fishing through my bag for my phone. "I saw Sal and he—"

"What is it?"

"Brandon." I frowned, hitting redial. My missed call log was maxed out. Brandon knew that I was in an exam and wouldn't call me if it wasn't important.

"*Taylor, seriously,*" Brandon said through the phone. "*You need to get to the hospital.*"

"What? Why?" I asked, resting my hand on my heart. "Jesse, oh gosh, it's Jesse."

"*He… he's, I don't know what's wrong with him, but he's in pain, just get here,*" Brandon murmured. "*Iris Cove Private.*"

"I know where he works," I breathed, blinking back tears as I hung up the phone. The pain, I could feel the pain, but it wasn't from the dying man, it was…

"Taylor?" Harper's urgent voice whispered.

"It's Jesse, I—"

He nodded. "I heard, I'll drive you. Where are you parked?"

"I, um… on the terrace, maybe?"

Harper wrapped his arm around me, leading me away from the sidewalk and down towards the esplanade. My hands were shaking, so I tucked my phone away and just focused on functioning.

"I should have known that it was him, why didn't I know?" I muttered as Harper drove. "I just thought that it was the guy from this morning, it made sense that it was… but Jesse…"

"What are you saying?" Harper asked. "What happened this morning? What did Sal do?"

I looked up and blinked. "He… I went to see him because

129

of the fire; I wanted to make sure that he was still around. But then someone was dying, so he took me, and I felt it, I was there…"

"He took you on a reap?" Harper frowned. "Were you seen?"

I shook my head. "No, I… we were linked, so I was invisible, but it meant that I felt it, the pain, everything, and I… it was the worst thing that I have ever experienced."

"And Jesse?"

I shrugged. "I only just found out about him. I don't know."

Harper was quiet for a moment, but I could see his mind ticking over. The silence was unnerving because I just wanted to know anything that might explain what was happening.

"What is it?" I breathed. "What are you thinking?"

Harper's brow creased. "You're linked."

"Hm?"

"You and Jesse are linked, you're twins," he mused. "The other day, when Sal took your pain away, he said he was sent home sick. He felt it too, the same thing at the Full Moon, he woke up with it, didn't he say?"

My hand rose to my mouth. "It's me, I'm hurting him. How do I stop it?"

"I don't know if you can, you can't control it," Harper breathed.

"But what if it kills him? He can't handle it the way I can – not the way he is, he's only human."

Harper gripped my hand. "I might be wrong. I… I might

130

be wrong."

I brushed the tears from my cheek. I'd done far too much crying today already.

My mum and dad, Charlie and Jack Mistry, were already there at the hospital when Harper and I arrived. Dad was talking to one of the doctors as only a concerned doctor-father would, and Mum was being comforted by Brandon. She looked up as I burst in, as eloquently as ever, and ran over to me.

"Taylor, honey," she gushed, wrapping her arms around me. "I'm glad you're here. We don't know what's wrong, but his body is reacting as if it's in pain. It's so strange, no one can tell why."

I glanced at Harper and bit my lip.

"Hello," Mum said, looking to him. "I think we may have met before when Taylor was in here. I'm Charlie, Taylor's mother."

Harper smiled politely. "I'm Harper Lovett. It's a pleasure to see you again, Mrs Mistry. Though I am sorry it is never under happy circumstances."

She nodded. "Please, call me Charlie. You're a friend of Taylor's, are you Harper? Taylor has been so busy lately. I'm a little out of the loop."

"Mum, Harper's my boyfriend," I murmured. "Can I see him? Jesse, I mean, where is he?"

My mother's eyebrows had lifted, but whatever she was thinking, she seemed to change her mind before she spoke it.

"Ashley is with him," she replied. "But Brandon will take you."

Brandon looked up and nodded. I leant in to hug Harper.

"Call Cole and see what he thinks about your theory, get him to check with Rob too, just in case," I whispered.

Harper lowered his head as I stepped back, then spun to follow Brandon to Jesse's room. It was a private room, as I expected, and the curtains around his bed were drawn. As I stepped through the doorway, I could hear the short bursts of breath that my brother took through his teeth. It sent a similar ache through me.

"Jess," I sighed. "Jesse."

Ashley was holding his hand as if it was the only thing keeping him alive. But when I stepped towards the bed, her grip seemed to weaken.

"Hey, Ashley," I said.

"I'm glad that you're here, Taylor." She pouted. "He needs you."

I swallowed and rested my hand on her shoulder, and she stood up. "I'll be right outside."

"You don't have to go."

She smiled, though it was almost a frown. "I'll be right outside. He needs *you*."

I bit my lip and replaced my hand in Jesse's as hers released. Brandon stepped back from the door as she stepped out. I climbed up beside my brother, my twin.

"Jesse, I'm here," I murmured. "I'm sorry."

His grey eyes looked unfocused as he looked at me. "Tay."

"Be strong, I need you to be strong," I whispered, feeling the moisture from my eyes bleed on the pillow. I squeezed his hand harder to try and give him some of my strength, but I only felt the weakness in his returning grip. His body flinched again.

"N-nothing w-works," he trembled. "It m-makes n-no s-sense."

"Don't try to talk." I pouted, shuffling closer so my forehead touched his. My mum used to say that when we were kids that she used to wake up in the morning and find that one of us had snuck in to sleep beside the other during the night. My father used to say that it was a twin thing that we felt like we needed to be close to each other because we had been for the nine months of gestation, well, eight and a bit.

His eyes closed and I felt him convulse again. Why wasn't anything working? I glanced up at the rapid heartbeat reflected on the beeping monitor and squeezed my eyes shut. This was all my fault. Jesse was in pain because of me, because I had been stupid enough, *yet again*, to flirt with the supernatural world. I never even dreamt that it would affect him. If I had, I never would have... would I have done anything differently? Harper's life for Jesse's? I shook my head and cursed fate. Everything was turning out so wrong. If only I didn't go to see Sal this morning then...

"Sal," I had barely mouthed the name when I reached around for my phone in my pocket. I'd made sure that earlier I had saved his number in my phone since I'd only given him mine before. I went to compose a new text and typed as quickly as I could.

"Something went wrong, twin brother in pain. ICPH. Help." Send.

I didn't know what he could do, or if he could do anything. I didn't know how the reaper thing worked, but I did know that he'd somehow healed a part of me last Monday, and Jesse was impacted by it. If he could only try and do the same to Jesse now, then I could deal with whatever came with it. I would deal with it.

I tucked the phone back and returned my hand to Jesse's, feeling the sporadic squeeze from him as the agony rippled through him.

"You're not alone," I whispered. "You're safe. Everything is going to be okay, Jesse. I'm here. Everything is okay, you're not alone, you're safe…"

My words were like a lullaby, constant and rhythmic. I could feel Jesse's grip weaken further, and I tried to keep mine tight to compensate, but before too long, mine began to weaken too.

*

"Taylor," a French-English accented voice said as my shoulder shook. "Taylor."

My eyes blinked open slowly to see Harper standing above me, but my hands were still tightly gripped on someone else's.

"Jesse," I gasped. "Jess? Jesse?"

His eyes were closed, but he was breathing. He was asleep, and seemingly more relaxed than he had been before I fell asleep.

"What happened?" I sighed, still staring at my brother.

134

Harper cleared his throat, and I looked over at him as he stepped back to reveal Sal.

"Hey, Taylor Mistry." He smiled weakly. "I got your message."

"Sal, you came."

"It sounded urgent."

I nodded. "What happened? Is he still in pain? Where are my parents, and Ashley, and Brandon?"

"Brandon and Ashley are in the café with your mother," Harper replied. "Your father is still talking to Jesse's doctors."

"Okay," I answered. "Were you right about… about Jesse and I being linked? Did I do this to him?"

Harper looked to Sal who frowned. "I don't know how it happened, but yes, it sounds like whatever you feel, your brother does too."

I looked down at Jesse, sleeping peacefully. "What did you do? Did you do anything? Did you take his pain away?"

"I didn't do anything." Sal shrugged. "I got your message, and after I figured out that ICPH meant Iris Cove Private Hospital, I came here. Wolfie was pretty confused to see me, but then I showed him your text, and he explained your little theory about being linked. The vampire was already here, so we sent the others for food, and here we are."

I glanced up at the monitors attached to Jesse, and they all looked like they were beeping normally. Reading them was something that I had learnt early on when my father used to bring Jesse and me with him to see his patients on the weekends.

135

"So, how did he get better then?"

"I guess you did that, Mistry," Sal replied. "Or it's a mystery, get it?"

I shot him a dark look that probably didn't have the weight that I was after. I was too relieved that Jesse seemed to be okay.

"What happens now?" I asked, directing the question at Harper. "I can't... he can't go through this every time I..."

"I don't know," Sal replied. I glanced at him, and his orange eyes widened. "Oh, not talking to me? Got it, Wolfie?"

"It's Harper," I corrected.

Sal smirked. "I know."

"I don't know either," Harper answered, ignoring our banter. "It's rather curious. Rob wasn't sure how much help the Weavers could be, but—" he fell silent as Jesse took a deep breath, appearing to stir. I looked back at the two boys and waved them away, and they both backed towards the door. I shuffled towards my brother.

"Jesse?"

He yawned. "Hey, I thought it was you."

"Of course it's me." I smiled. "How are you feeling?"

"Exhausted."

"Yeah."

His lips pulled up. "You look tired."

"So do you."

He frowned. "Do they know why it happened? Man, I've never felt anything like it. It must've been nerve pain because nothing worked to make it go away."

I shrugged. "I honestly don't know."

His hand lifted then fell on my arm. "I'm glad you're here, Taylor."

"Me too. I was really scared, Jess, really scared."

"I'm sorry."

"Don't you apologise," I whispered, curling up beside him. "None of this is your fault."

He exhaled. "I wouldn't call it anyone's fault, but I'm still sorry that I worried you. You had your exam today, how did it go?"

How was my brother so selfless when I was so selfish?

"It was fine," I lied. "I wish that I'd have known you were here though, I wouldn't have bothered with it."

"I'm glad you didn't know then," he replied. "I know how much passing means to you, especially after what you've been through in the past year. You've worked really hard, Taylor. I'd hate to mess things up for you."

Guilt seized me, strangling my trachea. "Jesse, if I messed things up, trust me, it's all my own doing."

"You're too hard on yourself, sis," he sighed. "You always have been."

"Maybe."

"Definitely."

"Jesse, darling, you're awake," Ashley said, sobbing. "Are you okay? I was s-s-so…"

I sat up, as she rushed over and flung herself on top of him. I took the opportunity of her distraction to slip off of the mattress. My mother and Brandon appeared in the doorway beside Harper, and I smiled and made my way over to him.

"Harper told us that Jesse was all right." Mum smiled with tears in her eyes. "You always could make each other feel better just by being there."

"I'm just glad that he seems to be okay now," I answered, taking Harper's hand.

"He had us all on edge for a while there." Brandon frowned. "I wish we knew why it happened so suddenly. The medical staff who were around him just said that he folded and started convulsing."

I cringed. "I… he… as long as he's okay now."

"It is weird though, you have to admit. Not the first time too, did he tell you—?"

"Yeah, he told me," I sighed. "It's a little weird, but I'm sure that there's some kind of logical explanation for it all."

Ever the scientist.

Brandon went in to sit beside Jesse. Mum followed, and I looked up at Harper.

"Did Sal say that Cole was here?" I whispered.

Harper nodded. "He needs to stay out of sight though. He worked with your father about twenty-years ago, so—"

"Oh." I blinked. "Okay, does he know anything? Does Rob?"

"Rob doesn't know a lot about non-Weaver beings, but he's willing to help where he can," he answered. "But a lot is going on with his foster son, Joel, right now so if we can get by without him…"

I nodded. "Well, Eden can still help, right? She's supposed to be super strong full-blood Weaver. Plus, she's dating

138

Brandon now, so I guess she'll be around."

Harper's eyebrows rose. "Really?"

"Uh, I've got to go." Sal frowned. "I need to be somewhere."

I shivered. "Okay, thanks for coming."

"Anytime," he murmured, his orange eyes panning from me into the room. He seemed to do a double take as he glanced at my family and friends, his brow drew, which sent a shadow over his eyes.

"What's wrong?" I asked, not oblivious to the fact that Sal could read lifespans as if they were written on people's foreheads. "Do you *see* something?"

Sal's head shook slowly. "Nothing. See you later."

He stepped back and spun on his heel, heading quickly down the white hallway. His black silhouette looked a little out of place against the brightness, but it was somehow fitting considering what he was. I looked up as another movement caught my eye.

"Dad," I sighed. "Anything?"

"Taylor." He smiled weakly. He stepped forward to kiss me on the head, and then looked up at Harper and extended a hand. "Jackson Mistry."

"Doctor Mistry." Harper nodded. "My name is Harper Lovett, sir."

"Harper, call me Jack," my dad said. "You the one who's been looking after my daughter, then?"

"Yes, sir."

"Jack."

139

"Jack," Harper amended. "Yes. Taylor's wellbeing is at the top of my list."

I frowned. "How did you know? Mum didn't even know."

"Jess mentioned something to me when he called for a consult." Dad smiled, his golden-brown eyes glinting. I'd always wished that my eyes were as golden as my father's, but they were more bronze-brown than gold like his.

"We've both missed you," he continued. "I thought you coming back from Italy meant that your mum and I would get to see you more, but we've hardly heard a peep from you since you and Jesse moved out."

I shook my head. "Sorry, Dad, I... I'm still trying to settle back into uni and everything. I'll be better. It shouldn't take Jesse being in the hospital for me to see you guys."

"He's awake?" Dad frowned. "His heart rate looks normal."

I shrugged. "I guess whatever it was passed."

My father ran his hand through his grey-flecked blond hair. "I should check on him."

"Okay."

"Are you going to stay?" he asked. "Don't you have exams?"

I shook my head. "They don't matter. Jesse—"

"Taylor, there's nothing that you can do. Besides, he seems better now."

"What time is it?"

"Eleven," Dad answered. "Go home. Harper, take her home."

"I'm not leaving him, Dad." I frowned, walking into his room to stand at the end of his bed. "Jesse wouldn't if it was me."

"Taylor, go home, I'm fine," Jesse croaked. "You have exams."

I shook my head and started to disagree again, but Mum stood and pushed me out the door.

"We'll call. We'll all call if anything changes. But Jesse will be fine now," she said. "Harper, you'll look after her, won't you?"

Harper started to nod, but I shook my head. "Mum, I really think that I should stay just in case—"

"In case what? Honey, there are doctors everywhere."

"But what if Jesse needs *me*?"

Jesse coughed. "Taylor, our unit is five minutes away. Go and get some decent sleep, they'll probably discharge me tomorrow anyway."

I looked at him and sighed, letting my eyes pan to my mother, Ashley, Brandon, my dad, and then to Harper, who slipped his hand in mine. There was no point in arguing. Clearly, they were all going to get me to leave because, apparently, Jesse was fine, and my education was important. Maybe Jesse was fine, and perhaps he would be as long as I kept my feelings in check and didn't participate in any more reaping.

"Everyone in this room will call me if anything changes," I said firmly. "Everyone."

They all nodded, maybe more to humour me than anything

else.

"Except me, if, well, you know." Jesse smiled.

"Not funny, Jess."

"Too soon?"

I shook my head and walked over to him squeezing him tight. "Be okay, Jesse, okay?"

"I'll be fine," he whispered. "Promise."

I nodded and stepped back; giving Mum and Dad a kiss goodbye before letting Harper lead me out the room.

"He will be okay, Taylor," he said.

"We'll see," I mumbled. "I guess if it was me that caused it, then I have the power to control it. I just don't want to think about how it will affect him come the next Full Moon."

Harper squeezed my hand. "I'm sorry that this is affecting your family."

I sighed. "Such is fate, right?"

"We don't always have to accept our fate."

"I don't see how we can turn this one around though." I shrugged. "I am what I am, and Jesse is my twin brother. Apparently, those two things don't go together."

"We'll figure out a way to make sure that they can," he replied.

"How?"

Harper's brow creased, darkening his usually light green eyes. "We get some sleep and see what our options are in the morning. Things always look brighter in the sun."

I rolled my eyes. "That is terrible."

"It's also true."

I stopped as we stepped outside and sucked in a breath of midnight air.

"Life is strange isn't it?" I whispered. "It can all change in an instant, and the next thing you know you're on a completely different path to the one that you thought you'd be on."

Harper nodded. "There have been a lot of changes lately."

"I don't know how to make them stop."

"I don't think you can," he replied. "But you can try and make them work for you rather than against you."

"How?"

"By not letting them defeat you, and by keeping your chin up until the next change comes along."

I bit my lip. "Is that what you did when you became what you are?"

"I didn't let it defeat me. It may control me physically, but if I know that it's coming, then there are certain variables that I can control too."

"Like where you are so you don't hurt anyone when you change?"

He nodded.

"But what happens if it doesn't matter where I am?" I asked. "Sure, as long as you, and Hunter, and even André now aren't around when I change, then that's all fine, but what if no matter how far I go, Jesse still gets hurt."

Harper's head dropped, and my heart sank. There was no answer; there was no pain for me without pain for him. As long as I was what I am, my brother would suffer for it. I couldn't live with knowing that my supernatural existence came with

143

that consequence, but the alternative, not living, that didn't seem like an option either. I didn't want to die, but I didn't want to cause the death of my twin. Surely that wasn't the only two ways that this could go for us, surely there was something else. I shook my head to clear it.

"Such is fate."

Phase Six

The Change

I nearly missed my morning exam the next day. At least if I had, then I might have a better excuse for failing. I couldn't concentrate, I was too worried about everything else that was happening that I couldn't control. It was stupid. But at least by the end of the three hours, I had filled in the blanks for most of the answers. I didn't know if it was enough, but it was all that I had in me, so it would have to do.

"Hey, Taylor, how did you go?" Brandon said as I opened my door.

I looked around the unit and found him on my couch with Eden. It irked me that he was here, and I wasn't sure whether it was because he was with her, or just because he was here.

"Is Jesse home?" I asked, ignoring him.

"He's resting."

"Oh." I nodded, heading towards his room.

"With Ashley."

I pivoted. "Oh."

"Hi, Taylor." Eden smiled. "Nice house, cozy."

"Hi, Eden. Thanks."

"So where's Harper? I thought you two were nigh inseparable in daylight hours."

Brandon huffed. "Lately in the night hours too."

Eden gave a laugh that made my cheeks blush. "Are unicorns extinct yet?"

"What?"

"Still none of your business, Eden," I sighed. "And he was spending some time with Hunter and André this morning. I'm meeting him soon."

"Ah, Hunter." She smirked. "I heard that she's a little catty. I can't wait to meet her."

I glanced at Brandon and was glad that he seemed to miss everything that we were saying. He was too busy playing with the straps on her singlet.

"So, are you two staying? Because if you are, then I'll go." I said.

Eden stood up. "I should go, I have things to do. Sorry to crash your place, Tay, home is a little tense right now."

"Harper mentioned." I nodded. "I hope everything is okay."

She smiled. "See you soon."

"Hey," Brandon squealed, crawling after her. She spun around and kissed him with so much zeal that I was a little surprised that neither one of them burst into flames. At least she was more than qualified to extinguish them.

"Later, kids." She beamed, closing the door behind her.

Brandon exhaled theatrically. "Damn."

"You know that she's older than us, right?" I asked, folding my arms. Older and would never physically age. It was a doomed relationship. Not that any of Brandon's lasted anyway.

"So?" He shrugged. "Isn't Harper older than you?"

"Yes, but that's a bit different."

"How?" He frowned. "Wow, you have so many double standards, Taylor. Or do you just have a set of rules that you live by and another set for everyone else?"

I blinked. "Excuse me?"

"Don't judge on looks, only girls can date older guys, I'm sure there are more."

"That's not even…"

"Whatever, no one asked you," he sighed. "I'm going. Tell Jesse that I'll see him later."

I pressed my lips together and nodded, feeling the slam of the door vibrate through me.

"Brandon?" Jesse's voice called.

"He just left, Jess, he said that he'll see you later," I said as his head peered around the corner. "How are you feeling?"

He appeared to shrug, but I could only see one shoulder. "Fine, just like normal actually, but they won't let me back at work until Thursday."

I nodded. "Rest up while you can maybe."

"Are you all right, Tay? How did the exam go?"

"I went." I smiled.

"When's your next one?"

"Thursday."

"Big day for us on Thursday then," he sighed. "Are you meeting Harper now?"

"Soon."

He nodded. "I, um, Ashley is here so…"

"Go, I'm fine," I replied, forcing a smile. "I'm just going to grab lunch and head back out."

Jesse straightened and continued to stare at me. I could see that he wasn't being fooled by my nonchalance, but didn't want to question me.

"I'm glad that you're okay, Jesse," I murmured. "I want you to stay okay… okay?"

He lifted his head. "Okay, you too."

It took us both a moment before we peeled away our separate ways, and after I'd made myself a salad sandwich for lunch, I sent Harper a message to meet me in the cemetery, in the Amund Tomb. It was the tomb where we had spent time hiding out when Harper first put together that I was being hunted by the wendigo. I wasn't crazy about the place then, and my opinion hadn't changed much, but it was the only place that I knew of where we could be alone, and no one would bother us. So, after gathering as many blankets as I had, I drove to the cemetery.

"*Bonjour.*" Harper smiled. "Are you all right?"

"Yeah." I nodded. "I just wanted to see you without all the other people around. I couldn't think of anywhere else where there would be no one."

His eyes twinkled with amusement. "That is very true. Good thinking."

I took a breath and let it out, reaching in to scoop my pile of blankets up.

148

"Did your exam go well this morning?"

"Not really. I mean, I think that I could have done better, but not this week," I sighed. "Not lately."

He walked over to me and took the blankets from my arms, throwing them inside the door, and then wrapped his arms around me.

"It's over for now. You only have a couple left, and then a well-earned break."

I hugged him tightly. "If we all survive that long."

"We will."

"I wish that I was as sure as you."

"I'll be twice as sure for the both of us then," he murmured, brushing his hand down my long brown hair.

"I don't know what's going to happen tomorrow, or next week, or next month," I whispered into his chest. "All I know is that right now I love you, and I don't want to be scared any more."

"I don't want you to be scared. We'll just take things as they come, and everything will work out fine."

"Okay."

He laughed. "Okay? I thought you'd need more convincing than that."

"I don't want to worry any more. I feel like I'm spending all my time worrying about what's to come, and I can't control it even if I tried," I murmured, stepping back. "All I can control is how prepared I am and what I do in the current moment. Sal can tell me about preparing later on, but *right now*, I just want to be here, alone, with you."

"And a pile of blankets."

"From memory, it gets cold in here."

He smiled. "Right, yes. I suppose you were cold last time."

I swallowed. "Or, um, maybe I thought that you could keep me warm, and we could, uh, just use the blankets as, like, cushioning."

He bit his lower lip. "Taylor?"

"Y-yes?"

"We are in a tomb."

My voice shook. "That's right."

"You want me to… keep you warm in a tomb?" He smirked. "Is that how you pictured it?"

I felt my cheeks burn. "I… if you don't want to—"

"I'm not saying no. Don't get me wrong, but I want to make sure that this is what *you* want."

I drew circles on his arm. "I didn't actually picture it… my first time to be with a werewolf either, I… so much has changed, I've changed, and the one thing that hasn't is that I always pictured it with someone that I loved and trusted, and someone who loves and respects me. I don't think I'll find anyone else in the world that is better for me than you are. So, no, maybe I didn't picture it in a tomb, but what better place to feel more alive than… here?"

Harper's face dropped slowly towards mine, then everything moved very fast – the way he scooped me up in his arms, the way he laid me down on the mountain of linen, and the constant flutter of my heart as it furiously pumped the heated blood around my electrified body. Then everything began to slow, his touch, his kiss, the way his fingers carefully peeled off my layers of clothing and ran down to the ends of my hair.

It wasn't how I pictured it, not at all, but then again, my imagination was never clever enough to dream up someone as amazing as Harper.

*

"Are you cold?" Harper asked, pulling his white T-shirt up over my shoulders. I shivered but shook my head.

Harper laughed. "No?"

"I'm warm," I whispered. "On the inside at least."

"And?"

"And… I can feel my heartbeat everywhere."

His lips pressed below my ear, and I felt the sensation tingle down my body.

"Anything else?" he sighed.

"Sore. Um, the ground is hard."

He sat back and bit his lip. "Did I hurt you?"

I frowned at some marks on his arms that looked like burns. "Did I hurt you?"

"I barely noticed."

My fingers traced them, resting my hands over the places where I'd obviously gripped him, and my nails seared his skin.

"I'm sorry."

"Don't apologise." He smirked. "At least you didn't break the skin."

151

I took a deep breath and let it out. "Will they heal?"

"As its silver, it will probably leave a scar."

"I'm sorry."

He shook his head. "Stop apologising, it was worth it."

I felt my cheeks burn. "It was."

"*Oui.*"

Harper shuffled, pulling another blanket out from beneath the pile, and wrapped it around me.

"One thing about tombs, no central heating," he said.

I looked around at the place that had once felt like a prison to me. "How did you know about this place? Did you know, um, Amund?"

Harper pressed his lips together, sitting forward to wrap his arms around his knees. I noticed that his back was burnt a lot worse than his arms, and would have felt a lot more terrible for it if I wasn't so embarrassed by it. But clinging onto him seemed more vital than life.

"I stayed here the first night that I arrived in South Coast," he answered, and I remembered that I had asked a question. "After you pulled the hunter's dagger from my shoulder when I was in wolf form. I came here to heal since not a lot of people visit cemeteries on Full Moons. A tomb is more protected than a gravesite, so I looked around. This one had more space than others, and offered more protection."

I propped up on my elbows and flinched at the pain the concrete caused. "Didn't you stay with Rob and Ebony?"

"Eventually." He nodded. "But not for the first night, at least. It took longer for me to change back into human form because of the silver injury, and they didn't know I was coming until I was here. It took me a while to track them down, their house isn't central since it's integral that they conceal their magic from humans. Plus, transportation is easy for Shadow Weavers."

I shuffled back and leant my back against the cold cement. "Fair enough. Had you met Rob before you came here?"

"Yes, as I said, transportation is easy for Weavers. He used to check in on me after my father was killed. They had forged a friendship when he lived in England as a firefighter."

"I remember you mentioning that he was a firefighter. Eden is one too."

He shrugged. "It's a common occupation for Weavers, like electricians really."

I nodded. "So what about your mum? I remember you saying that you lived in Brittany for a while growing up, and then moved to Derbyshire?"

"That's right," he murmured. "We moved to Brittany when I was four which was where *maman* grew up. She passed when I was twelve, so my father and I moved back to England."

"And you stayed there until your father passed away?"

His eyes tightened. "*Oui,* until he was killed. Then I went back to France for a while."

"To Paris?"

He smiled weakly. "*Oui.* I attended university there."

"So that's why you were in Paris to see me when I was there for the weekend," I said. "I thought it was odd for you to be in a crowded city."

153

"A crowd is easier to blend in. But, as you know, it is also easiest to feel lonely in."

I nodded. "What about siblings? You didn't have any brothers or sisters?"

"No, well, I had a little brother, but he was stillborn. My parents never tried for more children after that."

I pouted, reaching to brush my hands on his shoulder. He rested his hand on it then flinched. I let my hand fall.

"How is Jesse? Is he home from the hospital?"

"Yes, he was there with Ashley when I got home after the exam," I sighed. "He seems fine, normal as always, so I hope that he stays that way."

Harper nodded.

"How did things go with Hunter and André this morning?"

His nose wrinkled, it was cute. "There was no clawing."

"Good start."

"He is clearly smitten with her." He huffed. "He follows her around like a pet and, of course, she loves the attention."

"Do you think that maybe she likes him too?"

Harper's brow creased. "No, no. Not the same way. I have seen Hunter in love, and that's not it. She is just compelled by the company of another cat-shifter. She has not come across another in years since they're rare as they are born that way."

I frowned at the thought. "You've seen her in love with, um, do you mean with you?"

He shook his head. "She is not in love with him."

"Are they staying?" I asked after a moment.

"For a while, yes. At least until after the Full Moon. Hunter

154

has opted to stay with me during the change since Cole and Ruby will be with you."

"They will?"

"Yes. Since Sal said that banshees are not a threat to vampires, Ruby wanted to be with you as I cannot be." He smiled weakly.

I shuffled. "So, why doesn't Cole just go with you again?"

His eyes dropped. "Cole did not want to leave Ruby."

"He did last Full Moon. Oh. You mean, he didn't want to leave Ruby alone with me, just in case Sal was lying since he hates vampires."

"I know that you would never hurt your friend," he breathed, cradling my cheek in his palm.

"But it's not going to be up to me once I transform into a banshee."

"You still have one more to transition before you have to worry about that. Cole is just being over cautious. If I was him, and you were Ruby, I would not leave your side either, but my leaving ensures your safety from me."

"You mean, *your* safety from *me*," I mumbled. "I'm the threat now."

His eyebrow rose. "You do not look like a threat to me, especially like that."

I felt the blood rise to my cheeks as I glanced down at his shirt and the blankets that were covering me.

"Apparently, I'm more dangerous than I look." I smiled.

"Dangerous, yes. Threatening, no," he amended. "But I must say that if I am to die at anyone's hand, then I can only hope that it belongs to someone as lovely as you."

I frowned. "That's not funny, don't even joke about that. You're not allowed to die, and there is no way I'd kill you."

"I'm sorry," he whispered, leaning down to kiss my hand. "All I'm saying is that you are a charming angel of death."

"Angel of death," I said quietly. "You mean *screaming white woman of death*."

He shook his head, and the tip of his nose brushed mine. "No, angel."

I giggled and dropped my lips to his. "You're biased."

"I am in love."

"Same thing."

He breathed a laugh. "*Oui*, perhaps."

I smiled. "Do you think that we can stay here tonight?"

"In the tomb? I remember a time when you were bargaining to leave."

"Yes, well, it was more crowded then."

"*Oui*, true."

I exhaled then shivered.

"Are you sure you won't be more comfortable at home?"

My head tipped. "Maybe, but then we wouldn't be alone."

Harper glanced over at the concrete block. "Well, technically we are not alone here either."

I sighed and shuffled over to rest my head against his shoulder, and he wrapped his arm around me.

"Don't ruin the moment," I whispered, closing my eyes. "As far as I'm concerned it is just you and me."

He chuckled. "I like the sound of that."

His heart was racing in his chest, and it was the most vital sound and the most beautiful lullaby that I'd ever heard.

*

The next morning, Harper and I were awake as the sun came up. After getting dressed and piling all the blankets back into my car, we both made our way into *Clair de Lune* for breakfast. Even though I'd had little sleep, parts of my body still pulsed, and I still felt anxious for what was to come, I couldn't find it in me to care. So, I ate my egg white omelette, and sipped my espresso, and marvelled the incredible being sitting in front of me. I didn't feel very different after the night before, but I felt a lot of love for Harper. It was as if my life had been knitted together with his, and we were now whole, and neither would exist without the other. It was scary but amazing. I didn't want to lose it, and I was confident enough that it could not be lost without contest. We belonged to each other, and we belonged together. I knew just by looking at him that he felt exactly the same way.

I headed back to my unit after breakfast to have a warm shower and study for my exam the next day. Harper stayed, curling up at the end of the couch with his own book, while I took notes with mine.

"Ash, darling, you're going to be late," Jesse called from the kitchen table. He was sipping a coffee that I could smell from the lounge. Jesse took his coffee stronger than anyone I knew.

"I know, I... have you seen my phone, darling?" she said,

flittering past the opening to the hallway.

"It's charging in the kitchen."

She appeared, in a neat, trendy outfit and hurried towards it. "Right."

"You should use my charger, darling," Jesse sighed. "The one that you're using looks dodgy. I don't even think that it's a proper one."

"Darling, our phones are different models," she answered sweetly. "It's fine, it does the job."

"Drive safe," Jesse mumbled, tipping his head back so she could kiss him. "See you later."

"Bye, darling, have a good day."

I exhaled. "*Darling, darling, darling.*"

"Hey, quiet you," Jesse said. "Like you and Harper aren't just as bad."

Harper glanced up from his book and smiled at me, his olive-green eyes were glowing.

"We do not call each other little terms of endearment every three words." I sighed.

"Of course not." Harper chuckled. "*Ma chérie.*"

I laughed, and Jesse rolled his eyes.

"Oh, by the way, Brandon and I are going golfing today," Jesse said, standing and finishing off his coffee.

"How very exciting for you," I answered flatly.

"Harper, do you want to come? Or, you know, you can stay and watch my sister read."

Harper smirked at me then glanced over at my brother. "You're asking me to play golf?"

"Sure, if you want. What do you say?"

My eyebrows lifted as Harper's lips pressed together. I could see that he found the offer intriguing, even if he wasn't one to socialise. I liked the thought of Jesse and Harper getting to know each other, considering both were, and would continue to be, a large part of my life. The only spanner in this idea was Brandon, and what a tool he was.

"So?" Jesse prompted when Harper didn't reply. Harper was still looking at me with those wonderfully hypnotic eyes.

"You can say yes," I murmured, nudging him with my foot. "I'll just be revising anyway."

"I can stay," he offered.

"If you want to go, you should. It might be good for the two of you to do some male bonding."

Jesse exhaled theatrically. "Seriously, and you think Ash and I are bad. It's just a few hours."

I smiled weakly, and Harper nodded. *"Oui,* okay."

"You'll come."

"Yes."

"Awesome." Jesse smiled, giving me a wink. "We'll pick Brandon up on the way."

I caught Jesse's wrist as he passed, and was almost pulled off the couch.

"Hey, keep Brandon away from him, you hear?"

Jesse laughed. "Okay, but I think Harper can hold his own."

I glanced up at my muscled boyfriend and released my brother's arm. "Oh, I know he can. It's Brandon I'm worried

159

about."

Harper grinned his pearly grin and leant over me, practically pinning me to the couch.

"Je t'aime," he breathed. "I'll see you later, *ma chérie."*

I giggled. "Don't start."

His lips dropped to mine, and I felt my heart squeeze as I lifted my hand to his neck to hold him there. Jesse cleared his throat, and I remembered where I was and slowly let my hand drop.

Harper straightened. "Good luck with your books."

"Good luck with your cubs, um, I mean, clubs."

Jesse smacked Harper on the shoulder. "Right, let's go. Bye, Tay."

I lifted a hand to wave and watched them leave, mildly amused at how someone so paranormal could fit in so normally with my exceedingly normal and somewhat former life.

*

"Taylor," a voice whispered. It was dim in my room and colder than I was used to until I felt the warmth beside me.

I rubbed my eyes. "Harper?"

"Hi."

I turned and blinked up at him through the dark. "Are you just getting back now?"

"I'm sorry that I'm late, I wanted to say goodnight before I go."

"Go where?" I exhaled. "You don't want to stay?"

"You have an exam tomorrow. I thought you might want to sleep."

I reached for his hand and pulled on it, wrapping his arm around me. "I want you to stay."

He tightened his hold.

"Did you have fun with my brother?"

"Jesse is a remarkable person," he murmured. "But I would expect no less from someone who is related to you."

I smiled. "Well, if he's anything like me, then he must love you too."

"Not in the same way, I hope." He chuckled. "One Mistry is enough."

"Well, we're twins, so I think that is evidence that one Mistry is never enough."

I felt his lips at my neck.

"You are enough," he whispered.

I shuffled around to face him and ran my fingers down his cheek; his eyes seemed to glow in the darkness, like stars in a velvet sky.

"I never want this to change," I breathed. "Everything is changing, but I never want what's between you and me to change."

"It won't, I told you that I'm not going anywhere."

My head shook on the pillow. "I know, but what if we don't get that choice?"

"There's always a choice."

"Not when it comes to living and dying," I murmured. "That is a fate that tends to be set."

Harper pulled me against his chest, and his warmth made me shiver. "Not our fate."

"I wish that we could escape it, run away from it all, and just be a normal couple," I whispered. "We were sort of normal for a while, weren't we?"

"I don't think normal exists. Everyone just makes their own kind of normal, it's never the same."

"That's a sad thought." I pouted. "That our normal involves us turning into things that we can't control once a month."

His nose brushed my cheek. "If it means we can be together for the rest of the month, then I will duly pay that price."

I exhaled and rolled over, pulling his arm back around me. "I suppose we should just make the most of the time we have since it's all we can control."

"I agree," he breathed. "Now go to sleep, *ma chérie.*"

I breathed a weak laugh, and the shadows seemed to cradle me in their arms, along with Harper's, as I drifted back to sleep.

*

I seemed to focus better in my exam the next morning. My head was clearer, and I could concentrate on the science of what I was presented with. I felt grounded like I had somehow shifted back to the Taylor who was confident in what she knew, and what she could do. I felt like I knew who I was and what I wanted again, and like maybe everything might just work out. If

162

I was faced with a challenge, then I could deal with it, because I wasn't alone. I had friends again, I had Harper, and that was enough to set the spark of hope inside me into a blaze. The feeling continued into the weekend and rolled through until my last exam the following Tuesday. It was only after that was complete, marking my semester as complete, that I began to feel like time was working against me. I had until Saturday to wrap my head around the fact that after this Full Moon, I would change into someone or something completely different altogether. I would lose control over myself in the literal way, rather than the psychological way that I felt after losing the weight and transforming my life.

I met with Sal on Thursday afternoon, after his last exam, in the common room. It was pretty quiet there during the exam period, except for students clustering in there before they needed to report to the drill hall. Sal was more laid back than he had been on other occasions we had met, and I guessed it was because he had now completed his semester too, which meant a lengthy break before classes started again.

"What happens if you're in an exam and someone is dying?" I asked, rolling Sal's red apple between my hands. He was making his way through the second-last course of his five-course lunch, having already eaten cheese and crackers, take-out soup from *Excalibur,* and grilled beef with an Italian side salad.

He smiled down at his biscotti as he broke it in half.

"I ask to go to the bathroom and do my business, then go back and continue with it."

I rolled my eyes. "Your '*business*'."

"Death is a business." He shrugged, sipping on his espresso. "Sort of, I mean, I suppose I don't get paid for it, but it's a job."

I bit my lip.

"Are you hungry? Do you want some?"

"No, um, thanks."

"You don't eat much, do you?" he asked. "Or are you watching your womanly figure?"

I shrugged one shoulder. "I just lost a lot of weight, so I try to keep, um, a calorie controlled diet."

"Calories?"

"Not all of us have metabolisms like hummingbirds."

"Ruby-throated hummingbirds?"

I frowned. "How do you know the breeds of hummingbirds? I thought you were a philosophy major."

"Doesn't mean that I never studied science," he said. "Actually, there is a lot of psychology and scientific thought tied to philosophy. But yeah, I still studied biology in high school *and* paid attention. I just prefer to ponder general and fundamental problems over the periodic table."

"Whatever," I sighed. "So are we going to talk about what I came here to talk about?"

"Which is?"

"Quit it, Salvatore, you know what."

He bit off some biscotti, and I flinched as a crumb flew at my face. "Sorry, Taylor Mistry, it's a mystery to me."

"You are such a child."

164

He laughed. "Better to be young at heart than old."

I exhaled.

"So, you mentioned before that you got marked because you were saving the wolf from getting reaped, right?" he asked.

I nodded. "Harper got stabbed by a hunter's dagger, and I tried to help him. I guess I was in the way when the banshee came."

"That's sort of what happened to Alba too," he answered, finishing off his espresso. "She was the hunter though, and had just started hunting, so was unprotected. She got in the way of a banshee when they both went after the same shifter. Otherwise, banshees don't mark humans, like, ever. It's really rare that it happens. *Really* rare."

"Perfect," I sighed. "Of course it is."

"So, you saved the wolf, and killed the banshee, and now we're here?"

I frowned and shook my head. "There was a lot more to it than that. Actually, it took about a month for me to kill it."

"A month? What? It let you live that long?"

"Well, I was being hunted by a wendigo and severely cursed with bad luck in the meanwhile." I shrugged. "But after the others killed the wendigo, the moment Harper turned into a wolf he came after me too, but he managed to resist killing me… then the banshee showed up."

"Right, on the second night." Sal nodded. "The Full Moon night."

"No, it was the same night. The first one."

He pulled a face. "But how can that be if it wasn't a *Full*

Moon? Banshees don't change on Gibbous Moons, are you sure that the wolf didn't come after you on the second night, on the apex night?"

I shook my head. "No, it was definitely the first. Wait, are you saying that I could change on a Gibbous Moon night too?"

"No, banshees can't, not usually," he replied. "Alba was set on it being *just* the Full Moon, unless…"

"Unless?"

His head tipped. "Well, she seemed to change back when she finished her reap, so maybe because you were just marked, that meant she couldn't change back until you were, you know."

"Dead?"

He shrugged. "Maybe. It's just a guess."

"Well, your guess is as good as mine. You seem to know more about this than me."

Sal finally shoved the last of his biscotti in his mouth and started chewing. Mid-bite he stopped and looked up at me, and his frown seemed to darken his already dark features.

"Taylor, how many Full Moons did you say had passed since?"

"Two."

"As in, two *since* then?"

I blinked. "What do you mean?"

"Like, two have passed *since* you killed the banshee, as in the night after you killed it, then the one just gone," he clarified. "Right?"

"N… oh no," I breathed. I suddenly understood what he
166

was saying – the first one had passed the night after I'd killed the banshee, and then *two more* had occurred subsequently. Three in total had gone by, which meant that the transition phase was over. Come Saturday, I would begin the hunt as a full banshee.

"I suppose that explains why the last Full Moon made you crazy," he sighed, taking out a stick of spearmint gum and jamming it in his mouth.

I shook my head mutely.

"Well, hey, at least the worst part is over. Alba said the transition moons were the hardest," he said, pressing his lips together.

I looked up. "So, the hunting and killings after that were a piece of cake?"

Sal tried to smile. "Everyone likes cake."

I felt as if my lungs weren't inflating correctly, and my heart had risen to my throat. I had known that this was coming, but I thought that I'd have more time before it actually happened. Not that it would make a difference.

"Are you cool?" Sal asked, picking up the apple which had stopped rolling between my hands and flicking it at me. It rolled off the table and into my lap, and I caught it before it bounced onto the floor.

"*Cool?* Am I *cool?*" I snapped. "No, I am not *cool*. Nothing about this is *cool.*"

He sighed. "I was just asking."

"Hey, Tay," a cheery voice said, piercing my last nerve.

I looked up and rubbed my brow. "Hi, Brandon... um,

Eden."

"Hi, Taylor. Fancy seeing you here." Eden smiled. Her usually long red hair was cropped chin-length, and she wore navy blue trousers with a tight navy and red cotton shirt – her uniform. "Hey... not Harper," she added.

"This is Sal," I mumbled. "Sal, this is Brandon and Eden."

"What's up?" Sal smiled, shaking Brandon's hand before looking to Eden. His brow creased when he took hers. "Eden. I'm guessing... sparkie?"

"You don't look grim at all," Eden answered, her eyes lowering to the gum wrapper between Sal's fingers. She smiled as it burst into flames. "I'm a firefighter, but I can still make sparks fly."

Sal's eyebrows lifted. "I bet you can."

Brandon cleared his throat, and she released his grip.

"So what's going on?" Brandon asked. "Where's Harper?"

I looked up at him and saw the question was directed at me.

"He's with a friend," I replied.

"A friend? What friend?"

"He has other friends, Brandon," I snapped. "What's it to you? You don't even like him."

Brandon's blue eyes bulged. "I... he's all right, I mean, I'll admit that I'm not his biggest fan, but we had fun golfing last week."

"Are you okay, Taylor? You seem tense," Eden sighed a little condescendingly. "Perhaps you need to de-stress."

My eyebrows lifted as the heat rose to my cheeks.

168

"She's fine," Sal answered, poking me in the arm. "Exams get everyone on edge."

"But your last exam was Monday." Brandon frowned. "What are you even doing here?"

"Meeting a friend." I shrugged. "Your final exam was yesterday, so what are *you* doing here?"

Brandon tipped his head. "Meeting a friend."

"Do you know the one thing that I don't understand, Taylor?" Eden asked. I didn't actually want to know, but I had a feeling she'd tell me anyway.

"What is the one single thing that you don't understand, Eden?"

She smirked. "How do you have so many hot male friends, but still only stick to the one guy? I mean, *wow*, okay Harper is all kinds of yummy, but I mean, Brandon-blue eyes over here, and even *Signor* Sal—"

"Harper is more than enough for me," I answered flatly.

She pressed her lips together. "So, why are you so stressed?"

Sal stood up and grabbed my arm. "So, we're going to go."

"I hope it wasn't something I said."

"People to see."

I let him drag me away, knowing somewhere in the back of my buzzing mind that she was loads more powerful than I was. Even if my banshee abilities protected me from most things, I still didn't know to what extent it could shield me from electrocution, poison, or an inferno.

"Well, see you later, no doubt," Eden called. "And Taylor, I find that a good *scream* always makes me feel better."

Sal's hand tightened on my arm.

"Thanks for the tip," I answered. "Maybe you'll hear it Saturday night."

Eden laughed and then seemed to pale as she comprehended the threat behind my words. Brandon was still sitting there dumbly as Sal guided me out the door.

"Well, good luck marking a Weaver," he sighed, releasing me. "She was only kidding around with you."

"So why did you drag me away?"

"Because she's slightly obnoxious." He smiled.

I huffed. "Slightly."

"And that blond guy wasn't much better."

"Ugh, Brandon," I groaned. "I know. He's my brother's best friend."

"I remember seeing him at the hospital." He nodded, and then frowned.

"What?"

He looked up. "What?"

"What's that look again? That… look you get that gives me the chills." I shivered.

He shook his head. "Nothing."

"That's what you said at the hospital, but I know you saw something. Is it Brandon? Is he… is his number close?"

Sal exhaled. "It's nothing, Taylor, don't push it, okay? It's not for me to tell."

A wave of nausea hit me. "So you *did* see something. Sal, that's my family and… and friends you're talking about."

"I don't choose it. I don't even choose to see it, and I certainly can't change it, not even they can change it," he answered. "You'll see that come Saturday."

"Just tell me that it's not Jesse," I whispered, I could hardly get the words out. "Or my parents."

He stopped walking and sighed. "It's really not for me to tell. Besides, there were only two other humans in that room besides those three, and I don't want you going around thinking that someone's about to drop at any moment."

"How can you know this stuff and not warn people?"

"Because, believe it or not, most people don't want to know when they're going to die, it's a huge burden," he answered. "People live how they live. Deep down we all know we have an expiry date, so really we should all be living like it's our last day anyway."

I rolled my eyes. "How very philosophical."

He breathed a laugh and kept walking. I walked after him.

"Where are we going, Sal?"

"Oh, crap. I was just heading home. Where do you want to go? The library or something? The esplanade? *Clair de Lune*? *Excalibur*?"

"You're not still hungry, are you?" I frowned.

"I'm Italian, I'm always hungry."

I couldn't help but laugh. "You know, I actually lost my twenty-two kilos when I went to Italy."

He blinked. "*How*? Did you… how? Did you just not eat? But no one would let you *not* eat. Seriously, how did you do that? It's a mystery to me, Taylor Mistry."

171

"Gosh, you are so lame," I groaned. "And I guess I just ate in moderation, balanced the food groups, walked everywhere, ran when I could... yeah, I don't know. I did it, and it was easier there than it is here. Or maybe I just have more to think about being back, so I think less about what I eat. I've put back on some of the weight since being back."

"Well, I don't know what you used to look like before Italy, or even when you left there but, I mean, you look pretty great now, so I wouldn't worry about that stuff." He shrugged. "You only live once, so I guess it's good to be healthy, and you are. But as for the rest of it, don't punish yourself for people who don't even care what you look like at the end of the day, and if they do, they need a hobby."

"True." I smiled. "And sometimes I believe that too. But there are other times when I get so frustrated at myself for not being more disciplined so I can be as I was when I got back from Italy."

"For what?"

"What?"

"Or for whom?" he asked. "Does the wolf not like you as you are?"

I shook my head. "He loves me as I am. I guess it's just me who has a hard time sometimes."

Sal shrugged. "Well, only you can fix that one. Nothing anyone else says will make you see things how they see it."

I nodded. At least he understood. Even Jesse would go blue in the face sometimes trying to convince me that I was okay as I was.

"So, *Excalibur*?" he asked. "It's about time for some kind of fruit juice. You can have, um, water, or tea, or whatever you have."

"Black tea or black coffee."

"Like the Italians have it." He smiled. "How long were you in Italy for?"

"A year."

His eyebrows lifted. "That's decent That's more than I've spent there for any length of time. I went back for about a month after high school, then did a bit more of Europe. But since I didn't have a lot of money, I had to come home after about three months away."

We found a table outside at *Excalibur* and sat down.

"So you grew up in South Coast?" I asked.

He nodded. "But I don't have family here any more. My parents moved out here with my Nonna and Nonno, my mum's parents, just before I was born. We took a trip back to visit the rest of my family after my brothers were old enough."

"You have brothers?" I asked. "How many?"

"Had. Two."

I closed my eyes. "Oh gosh, I'm so sorry. I—"

"It's okay, relax."

"No, but I even knew that. I mean, you said that your family… the fire."

He drew in a breath. "Yes, but I never mentioned who my family consisted of."

"That… that's the most horrible thing in the world, I can't even imagine…" I shook my head. "How much younger were they?"

"Five and three."

"You were seven, right?"

"Seven." He nodded.

"So, what happened to you after they died? Where did you stay?" I asked, and then realised it was a completely personal question. "Sorry, you don't have to answer that."

He smiled weakly. "I lived with a few different families that took me in... but I was handed off a few times because the people thought that I had disciplinary issues."

"Gosh."

"It was a while ago, but I guess it doesn't get any easier. You just start to forget, and that just seems to make it harder. Childhood is hard enough without having a family, and then having to ease suffering and save souls." He laughed lightly. I felt a new sense of awe for the fact he was so well adjusted considering what he'd been through. I'd thought that my life was tough, my charmed life, but it was *nothing* compared to Sal's. I really was faced with first world problems.

"You're pretty incredible," I sighed.

His head tipped. "How you flatter me, Miss Mistry."

I rolled my eyes. "I just meant that you... you're a decent person, and some might have used that all as an excuse to be a bad person."

"I can't afford to be a bad person. You can't empathise with someone who is dying and be spiteful at life. Life is a gift, and if it weren't for the suffering, most wouldn't choose to give it up."

I shook my head incredulously. "Seriously, you... you're..."

"All right, enough flattery." He chuckled. "Tea or coffee? My shout."

"You don't have to—"

"Don't pity me, Taylor. Let me buy you coffee."

I exhaled. "Coffee it is then."

He nodded and then paused mid-step. "So, I'm going to be *right* back, but think about what kind of coffee you want, long, or short, or whatever, okay?"

"Forgot your wallet?"

Sal's eyebrow lifted. "I'll be right back."

I nodded and watched him run across the one-way street into the building where the student housing was. The second he was out of sight, my thoughts grew very loud. Tomorrow would be the night before the Full Moon and Harper would be gone, but not for my protection, for his. I thought that I had more time to prepare myself, but how could I? How could I wrap my head around the fact that in two night's time, I would be hunting him or someone like him? How could that ever feel right, like Sal said that it would? And what would that mean for Jesse when I changed? What if it landed him back in hospital, or worse? I wasn't ready. I wasn't sure if I would ever be ready for this, but there was nothing I could do to stop it. There was no way that I could control it.

"Hey, sorry." Sal whispered, shaking out his hands. "I... yeah, did you, um... hey, are you all right? You look sort of pale."

I tried not to think of the irony that thinking about turning into a screaming white woman was turning me white.

"I'm… I'm scared. I'm scared to change," I murmured. "What if I hurt Harper on Saturday night? What if his time was up with the last banshee and I have to finish the job? She tried, she tried to kill him, and he was dying, but he got saved, he got saved, and now I'm scared that it'll be me who needs to finish the job."

Sal frowned and sat down beside me. "Calm down."

"How can I calm down, Sal? How?" I sighed. "Do you know how scary it is to even consider the fact that I could have to watch someone that I love die? It was bad enough the first time. I don't think I can do it. I can't, I won't."

Sal looked around. "You can't stop it, Taylor. If it's his time, then there's—"

"Don't say *nothing*… don't say there's nothing that I can do."

His shoulders dropped. "You can't control everything, Taylor. Change and death are the only certainties in life."

"Love, that's a certainty too."

"Only until death," he whispered. "You can only love someone to death."

I frowned. "How can you say that? You of all people. You don't believe that love lasts… forever?"

"Nothing lasts forever. Or nothing should last forever."

I shook my head. "Sal, you're wrong."

"Maybe I am." He shrugged. "But that doesn't change the fact that death is unavoidable."

I exhaled in defeat because he was right. No amount of arguing would change the fact. Such is death.

Phase Seven

The Full Moon

"I don't want you to go, but I want you to go," I mumbled into Harper's chest. "Far, far away so nothing can hurt you, especially me."

"We will get through this," he whispered. "Whether you're a full banshee or not."

I hugged him tighter. "It makes sense that I am. Sal is right, three have passed, and now it's screaming white woman for me each Full Moon."

"We don't have to go tonight; we can stay here together, alone."

I shook my head. "We told Ruby we'd be there."

Ruby had decided to throw a little party of sorts, to bring everyone together before we all broke apart. I wasn't sure if it was because she didn't expect us all to survive the weekend, or whether she knew that we were all apprehensive about it, so were better off all being together. Whatever it was, Harper thought that it was a good idea, so did Cole and André. Apparently, it was only Hunter and me who were sceptical, but as soon as she heard that I agreed with her, she changed her mind. My main concern was that the majority of the people I'd be gathering with were potential suspects on my hit-list. I really would have preferred that they used the time travelling away from me, even if the company would be a good distraction for what was to come.

"We will still have the night together. I'm not leaving until sunrise," he whispered. "But we had better leave soon, or else we will be late."

"Okay."

When we arrived at Cole and Ruby's apartment building, Hunter and André were already there. I wasn't sure if Eden had been invited, but I hoped that even if she had been, that she wouldn't show up. Dealing with Hunter's attitude would be hard enough without Eden's remarks.

"Well, we're all here." Ruby smiled as we walked in. "Can I get you a drink, Harper? Taylor?"

"Water is fine," Harper replied. "Thank you."

I nodded. "Yes, water is great."

My eyes traced to Hunter and André who were sitting quite close on one of the Chesterfield couches. Hunter barely looked up from drawing circles in André's palm, but André greeted us both with a smile.

"All here?" Cole asked, appearing out of nowhere – vampires were quick and silent movers. "You didn't invite the grim, Ruby?"

"He declined my offer," Ruby sighed. "Something about *vampire territory*."

I rolled my eyes, and Harper shrugged out of his leather

jacket, and then straightened his V-neck T-shirt.

"*Dios mía*," Hunter muttered. "Harper, what happened to you?"

Harper blinked as she stood and hastened over, grabbing his arm and scrutinising the burns that my nails had caused.

He pulled his arm away. "Nothing."

"*Nothing*? You were burned. You are scarred."

"I said that it's nothing, so it's nothing," he answered firmly. Whether he meant to or not, his eyes flashed to me, and I felt my cheeks flush as my hands turned over in my lap.

"Ah, *nothing*," Hunter sneered. "Because *she* is nothing. Did she do this to you? Cole said that her nails are embedded with silver."

Harper's frown deepened, and I thought that I heard a low growl rumbling in his throat.

"I… it was an accident," I answered. "I didn't mean to—"

Hunter glowered at me. "You *never* mean to hurt him, but he always ends up hurt because of *you*. The two of you are *not* compatible, you are a disaster together."

"Hunter, stop. Enough," Harper barked. "No one asked for your opinion."

"You are a masochist if you stay with her, Lovett," she snapped.

"*Ma chérie,* you cannot make his decisions for him," André whispered, hugging her from behind. "He is a grown man who is in love, leave them be."

"Harper knows nothing of love, he… he is incapable of it," Hunter muttered, her olive skin flushed with fury and something else – arrogance? I stepped over beside Harper who instinctively wrapped his arm around me and pulled me against his side.

"You're wrong," I said. "He can love, and he does love. Why can't you accept that? Why won't you accept me?"

"Because *you* are all wrong for him. Harper needs someone who understands him."

"I do."

"You *think* you do."

"It is no use reasoning with her," Harper murmured. "You don't need her acceptance."

Hunter flinched. "After everything we have been through. I am simply looking out for you, Lovett."

Harper looked up, his expression exhausted. "I never asked you to. Now please, I do not want to fight with you, can we just try and at least *pretend* to all get along for one evening? Ruby and Cole have gone to the trouble…"

I pressed my lips together and glanced over at Ruby and Cole who were graciously hosting us all and, yet again, we were being horrible houseguests.

"The sooner dawn is here, the better." Hunter exhaled. "I will give you this one evening."

"How kind," I sighed. Harper's finger brushed my lips. "Sorry."

Hunter scoffed, and Ruby sighed.

"Water," she said, holding out two glasses towards Harper and I. "Shall we sit?"

The evening was relatively uneventful after that. Hunter

barely spoke, but I felt her dark cat-like eyes sneering at me for most of the night. I knew she didn't like me, that had been evident since Harper asked for her help to protect me months ago, but I thought that somewhere along the line we had turned a new leaf. After all, she had nearly been killed trying to protect me from the wendigo, but it only occurred to me now that it was more for Harper's benefit than mine. Even though she and André were always linked somehow, Harper had been right to believe that she did not love him the way he did her. He looked at her as if he was seeing the sun for the first time; she looked at him as one might consider a brother. There was the odd occasion through the night when I saw that look of love in her eyes. It twisted inside of me because it was only evident when her eyes regarded Harper when she must've forgotten that anyone else was in the room. It was selfish of me, but I resented the history that she and Harper shared. It was obviously more than the downplayed version that he had given me. It was more than physical, at least for Hunter, and even that was uncomfortable for me to consider.

Another thing that was uncomfortable was talking about what Sal had realised earlier in the afternoon that my transformation would occur this Full Moon, in two night's time. It didn't seem to change the plans much though. Harper would still leave with Hunter and André tomorrow morning, and I would stay with Cole and Ruby since they were the least at risk from my transformation. No one else really seemed concerned that the deadline had been moved forward a whole month. However, everyone was convinced that if Harper,

Hunter, and André made themselves scarce, the only person it really affected directly was me. I hoped that they were right, even if talking about it before it happened only made me more anxious about it actually happening. Regardless of whether my companions were on my hit list, it didn't negate the fact that I *would* have to hunt someone and mark them with death. I had tried not to think about it after leaving Sal and telling Harper, but the constant reminder kept the worry fresh in my mind.

As the night wore on, and as midnight struck on the grandfather clock between us all, I felt this strange coolness rattle through me, as if my bones were being chilled. I squeezed my eyes closed, and when I opened them again, everything seemed brighter – every*one* seemed brighter. I looked around at my friends and gave a small gasp as I noticed that they all seemed to be illuminated in varying degrees. Cole and Ruby had a dull glow, Hunter's was a little brighter while André seemed to shine, Harper's was also bright, but seemed to flicker. I didn't know what any of it meant, but I was too afraid to question it.

"Taylor? Are you all right?" Cole asked, noticing my obvious confusion. My eyes moved to his, and I nodded. He leant forward. "Are you sure?"

"Do I not look okay?" I murmured.

He frowned. "Your eyes are paler."

Harper looked down at me and tipped my chin up towards him. "Slightly, very slightly."

"What does that mean?"

Cole glanced at the clock. "Perhaps your body is preparing

itself for the change."

"But I still have another two days. Two nights before I… anything happens," I said. The brightness was giving me a headache so I rubbed my temples.

"Maybe I should take you home," Harper offered, helping me to stand. "It's after midnight, and I have an early start tomorrow."

"That's probably a good idea." Ruby smiled. "Get some rest, Taylor. It's been a long day for you."

I smiled humourlessly. "How long has your day been? When is the last time you slept, Ruby?"

"Oh, several years ago." She laughed. "I'll see you tomorrow."

I nodded, and Cole smiled at me.

"Good night to the both of you," he said.

"Good night," I replied, glancing over at Hunter and André. "Good night to you guys too."

André beamed, literally and physically, and stepped forward to give me a gentle and slightly awkward squeeze, considering Harper wouldn't let go of my hand.

"*Bonsoir, chérie* Taylor," he murmured. "Worry not; we will take care of your Harper."

Hunter huffed, and I stepped back.

"Thank you, I know you will," I replied.

Harper pulled me back to his side and said his own goodbyes before we both made our way back down to his motorbike in the basement.

"Are you sure that you're okay?" he asked as he handed me

184

the helmet. "Does your head hurt?"

I shrugged. "A little, I'm sure it will pass."

His fingers brushed my cheek as his olive-green eyes bore into mine. I could see the concern in them, which was my driving force behind keeping the reasoning for my headache from him. It was nothing that he could help, and I knew that he would only worry, or insist that he leave me earlier than dawn. I would do my best to ignore it until morning. The Full Moon would not steal any more of my time with Harper than it already was.

We went to bed almost immediately after we got back to my unit. Jesse wasn't there, so I guessed he was working nights which was good. I hoped that he was working when the Full Moon came, just in case it affected him in the same way that it had last time when it affected me. If we were linked, and this was bad, I needed him to survive it. If Harper was my heart, Jesse was my soul, and I couldn't live without either of them.

I could feel Harper's heartbeat against my back, strong and vital, and although it's thumping was like a serenade, I couldn't sleep.

"Harper?" I whispered.

"Mm?"

I looked over my shoulder and saw that his eyes were closed; the phantom light surrounding him still flickered.

"I can't sleep, can you?"

His eyelids lifted. "Not really."

"Are you scared too?"

"Not scared," he answered. "I am concerned for you. I

wish I could help you, I wish that I didn't have to go—"

"But you do have to go," I sighed, rolling over to face him. "You need to think of your own safety so you can come back to me in one piece."

"All I care about is your safety."

"And all I care about is *you*. I love you. I hate this, but I love you," I murmured. "So, even though I hate this, I hate that you *need* to leave, I need you to go because I love you more than I hate this."

He nodded. "You will be okay, Taylor."

"We'll see."

He smiled, brushing my cheek with his warm hand. "If I have to live, so do you."

"I think I said that to you once."

"I remember."

I frowned. "I think you were a wolf though."

"And dying."

"How do you remember that?"

"I remember a lot of things you say," he whispered. "Especially when you told me that when I left you before, I took your heart with me. I hated leaving you, and I hate leaving you for exactly the same reason. I feel like my heart now belongs to you, and without you, it doesn't beat for me, it only beats for you."

For some reason, my words, the words he was saying sounded infinitely better in his French-English accented voice. I swallowed back tears and pulled him towards me, kissing him as if it was the last kiss we'd ever share. My heart inflated and

186

felt like a grenade in my chest, ready to explode with affection for this one person that seemed too wonderful and too surreal to be real.

I wasn't scared any more, I would never again be afraid to be close to Harper, to have his hands move over me and his lips brush my skin because he loved me and he accepted me for who and what I was. To have him close to me, moving with me and against me, felt like the most natural and necessary thing in the world.

*

Harper slipped out early. I woke up from my restless sleep to his lips on mine, and because I knew that it was the start of my days without him, I couldn't get back to sleep. So I got up, made my scrambled eggs and oat bran porridge, and put on the television. I hadn't watched it in what felt like months, so whatever was on felt foreign to me. Instead, I occupied myself by playing with Raven for a while, until the front door opened.

"Taylor, you're up early."

I looked up and smiled. "Hey, Jesse. You too."

He glanced at the clock and breathed a laugh. "I just finished work. What's your excuse?"

"I guess I couldn't sleep."

He nodded and frowned. "Hey, are those the scratches from months ago? I thought they healed."

I turned my head to look at my shoulder, and they were almost glowing red. "Guess not."

187

"Are they sore? They look sore."

"No." I shrugged. "Hey, did you say that you just finished work? Are you working this weekend, say, tomorrow night?"

If Jesse was at the hospital when the Full Moon was at its apex, when I changed, then at least he'd be close to medical help if it was required.

"Saturday night?" Jesse's forehead wrinkled. "No, not Saturday night. I'm working tonight though. Why? Are you planning something? Do you want the place to yourself?"

I shook my head. "No, nothing. I am actually going out, but I... was just wondering what you were doing."

"Ash and I will probably stay in if you're out," he answered. "But don't feel like you need to go out. You're welcome to join us if you want – you and Harper."

I exhaled. "Thanks, but Harper has gone away with some friends for the weekend."

He tipped his blond head and yawned. "You can still stay."

"It's fine, I have plans." I smiled, standing and walking over towards him. Jesse blinked as I wrapped my arms around him and squeezed tight. His hand lifted to my back.

"Is everything okay?" he asked. "You're okay, aren't you?"

"I love you, Jess."

His chin rested on my head. "Taylor, you're scaring me."

"I'm fine, everything is... fine," I sighed. "I just miss you sometimes."

"I'm always here."

"I know, but I still miss you."

"I'm not going anywhere," he answered hugging me tighter.

188

"Except maybe bed, since I've just been working for twelve hours straight."

I laughed and stepped back. "Okay, I'll leave you to sleep. I might go and visit Ruby."

"Ruby." He nodded. "Am I ever going to meet her? You seem to hang out with her a lot, but never here."

I hated lying to Jesse. Hated it.

"She's sort of shy," I replied, it wasn't really a lie. "Plus, I never know when you're in, or out, or sleeping, so it's safer just to hang out at her place."

"This is your place too," he sighed. "Besides, when I'm tired, I'm practically the living dead. I can sleep through almost anything."

Almost. Except extreme pain.

"I'll invite her over soon then." I smiled. "I'm sure she'd love to meet you, she's heard a lot about you."

He laughed. "No pressure or anything."

"Never."

"Morning, sis, love you."

"Night, bro, love you more."

I waited until I heard his door close and then went to my room to change before heading out. Despite Jesse's claims of *sleeping through anything*, I was lousy at staying quiet on purpose, so I decided that a visit elsewhere was the safest bet to ensure he got a decent sleep. I didn't know where to go, I didn't know if Ruby was home, or if she was at *Crescent*, so instead, I headed over to the vet to see if they needed help. With exams being over, my days were suddenly wide open.

They let me stay and help out for a few hours which was good because by then it was about lunchtime, so I headed into town to *Clair de Lune* to get something to eat. Even though the quaint French-looking café was on a quiet side street, it usually managed to attract quite a few customers. Today was the quietest I'd ever seen it, and that was probably owed to the fact that exams finishing up meant fewer people in town.

"Hey, stranger," a voice said as a shadow cast over me.

I peered up through squinted eyes. "Eden. Hi."

"What'cha doing all on your own?" she asked. "No more hot guys to rub shoulders with?"

"You know what day it is."

"Friday?"

I exhaled.

"So, what? Harper's gone for the, uh, weekend," she sighed. "What happened to that Sal guy?"

"Sal is just a friend."

She shrugged. "Exactly, so why sit alone?"

"I enjoy my own company."

"Why?"

I frowned. "Some people are intolerable."

She nodded. "The grim is a little obnoxious."

"Funny." I smiled, taking a sip of coffee. "He said the same about you."

Her eyebrows lifted and she sat down. "No, he did not."

"Afraid so."

"What a jerk. I am so not obnox—"

I pressed my lips together and looked down at the table.

"You are!" she snapped, sending a spark upwards to burn a little hole in the material umbrella above us. "Frizzle."

"You okay?"

Eden sighed. "I don't have a lot of friends, okay? Before Ruby, I only really hung out with my brothers and their friends, so I've always been more comfortable around guys. I'm not obnoxious. I just don't know how to be friends with girls. Ruby is my first, sort-of, female friend."

I smiled.

"Right, laugh it up."

"No." I shook my head. "I just... I'm sort of the same, but in reverse. I mean, I have my brother but before, well, this year, I never really felt comfortable around guys so, it's strange to think that now I not only have a boyfriend but guy friends too."

She pulled a face. "Are you for real? You're not just trying to make me feel less pathetic?"

"Is that what I'm doing?"

"Apparently not consciously."

I laughed. "Okay, but yes, I am, um, *for real.*"

"So you and your brother, huh? Do you just have the one?"

"Yes, my twin."

"Twin?" She huffed. "I have twin brothers."

"Really?"

She nodded. "For real."

"Are they as obnoxious as you?"

"No, well, Raphael is." She shrugged. "He's a real hothead, pardon the pun, but Xavier is rather logical and level-headed.

191

More Zen, you know. They balance each other out as twins generally do. Is your brother all selfless and stuff then?"

My eyes widened. "I'm sorry, what? Selfless?"

"Yeah, since you're, you know, not."

"Excuse me?"

Her dark eyes rolled. "Come on, Taylor, you are a danger to Harper, and Hunter, and her little cat friend, and probably Cole and Ruby too if we were all smart enough not to take grim at his word," she explained, "in addition to that, didn't your brother end up in hospital because of you?"

"I couldn't… I can't help any of that." I frowned.

"You can help some of it," she said. "Maybe not the brother thing, but as for the rest—"

I leant forward. "I'm nearly indestructible and, from what I know of banshees, as one dies it's replaced with another. If I leave, that won't save anyone. I'm not selfish in staying, or asking Harper to stay. Sometimes when it's your time…"

I stopped and straightened, I was beginning to sound a lot like Sal, and it frightened me. It also scared me to think that wherever Harper went, he wouldn't be safe if his days were numbered.

"What?"

"Nothing," I mumbled. "I just can't help what I am any more than you can help what you are."

"I was born this way, you became that way because—"

"Because I saved Harper, and got marked with death," I finished for her. "How is that selfish?"

She shrugged. "Guess it isn't. Raph has his occasional

192

moments of logic."

"You know, being a twin doesn't mean you're half a person. It links you with them, but it doesn't stop you from having your own characteristics that have nothing to do with being opposite of the other."

"I should introduce you to Xav. I think you two would get along really well."

"I'm with Harper."

"Well then." She smiled. "Consider it another hot guy friend for you."

I blinked. "That's your brother you're talking about."

Her head tipped. "What can I say? He has good genes."

"You really are obnoxious, you know," I sighed, taking another sip of coffee. Eden reached for my mug, and I moved it away from her.

"And you really are selfish."

I felt the corners of my lips twitch into a smile as Eden's did the same, and then we both were laughing for no reason but the fact that we had seemed to have come to a strange kind of mutual respect between us.

I left a little after finishing my coffee and went home for a while before I headed over to Ruby and Cole's apartment building. Brandon was lounging on my couch, as per usual, with my cat, Raven.

"Hey," I said.

He peered up at me from behind his hand that shielded his blue eyes. "Oh, hi, Taylor."

"What's wrong with you?"

193

"I think I have a brain tumour."

I laughed. "That's a bit dramatic. Bad headache?"

"The worst."

"Drink too much last night?"

Brandon groaned. "I've cleaned up my act lately, you know that, Tay."

I shrugged.

"What are you doing now? Want to hang out?"

My eyebrows lifted. "Hang out with you?"

"Jesse is still asleep," he mumbled. "And your cat doesn't respond to my questions."

I glanced down at Raven and saw she was fast asleep on his chest.

"Are you going to be here all weekend?"

He smirked. "I can be."

"Great, can you make sure that she gets fed? I'm going to be out, and she seems to like you more than she likes Jesse."

"You want me to babysit your cat while you go out with your boyfriend? Ouch, times have changed."

"I'm not going out with Harper, he's away for a couple of days," I sighed. "I'm staying with a friend."

"April?"

"April isn't really a friend any more."

He exhaled. "Right."

"If you're not going to be here, then I'll ask Jesse, but you *always* seem to be here so…"

He sat up, cradling Raven to stop her from falling. She stretched and yawned, but didn't move.

"I can take care of her; my head is so bad that I don't think I'll be moving for a few days. Best to stay near a doctor just in case, you know."

I frowned and walked over to kneel beside him, pressing my fingers on his forehead. "Is it really that bad? You didn't hit it on anything, did you? Are you drinking enough water?"

Brandon's lips mashed together. "Are you worried about me?"

"I'm concerned, not worried," I answered, sitting back on my heels. "If you're going to look after my cat, I need you to be well enough."

"Is that it?"

"Is what it?"

"Is that the only reason why you… why you're concerned?"

I stood up and sighed. "What other reason would there be?"

"Maybe, I don't know, you care about me?"

I shrugged. "Sure, I care as much as I would care about anyone who was important to Jesse."

"But not you?"

"Brandon."

"I know that you're with Harper now," he said, rolling his eyes. "But—"

"There are no buts," I sighed. "I am with Harper, and that's not going to change. Besides, you're with Eden—"

He shook his head. "Not any more."

"Since when? I just saw her, and she didn't mention anything."

195

"Why would she? I broke up with her and, no offence, but why would she tell you? You didn't seem that close."

"Why did you break up with her?"

He shrugged. "Wasn't feeling it."

"You weren't?"

"Or she wasn't," he mumbled. "She flirted with a lot of guys, like that Sal guy, right in front of me."

My eyebrow lifted. "I can't imagine what that feels like."

He frowned. "You and I were never officially dating. I don't do that when I'm with someone for real. I might date a lot of girls, but I do it one at a time, when I don't feel it any more, I move on. They always know where I stand."

"Whatever."

"Whatever nothing, I would have been that for you," he sighed, lying back down. "I wanted that with you, but you were too condemning and judgemental of me to give me a chance."

I exhaled. "Well, it's all a matter of timing, you didn't want me before, and I didn't want you after. It had nothing… it wasn't because I… look, the timing was off, that's all. Besides, you and I can't even have a conversation without fighting… but none of that matters anyway, because I'm with Harper now, and like I said, that's not going to change."

His hand rested on his head again. "Okay, Taylor."

I bit my lip. "Anyway, I'm heading out in a bit so, um, I hope that you feel better."

"Thanks."

"And thanks for looking after Raven."

"Anytime."

"And, um, make sure that Jesse stays home tomorrow night."

Brandon frowned up at me. "Why?"

"It's, um, been a strange week or so for him, so I guess rather than going out like you guys usually do, a quiet Saturday night might be called for."

"Well, that's his call," he sighed. "But I'm pretty sure he intends to keep it low key for the same reason."

I nodded and went to my room, grabbing the bag that I had packed this morning for my weekend with Ruby, and headed back out. On my way, I stopped by the bathroom and wet a clean hand-towel to rest on Brandon's forehead. He flinched from the cold but exhaled.

"That feels good."

"Keep your fluids up and try not to take too many painkillers," I murmured. "Sometimes massaging your, um, temples helps too."

"You're an animal doctor."

"Not yet."

"Do dogs and cats work the same as people?" he asked. I thought of Harper and Hunter and pressed my lips together.

"Kind of." I shrugged. "But I grew up with people doctors."

"Right." He smiled. "Thanks, Doctor Mistry."

I rolled my eyes. "Please."

"Will I see you again? Or are you staying out for the weekend?"

"You'll see me again, you goof," I sighed. "But yes, I'm

staying out this weekend."

"Have fun."

I nodded. "Take care."

"Bye, Tay."

I closed the door and shook my head incredulously. Unwell boys could be really dramatic.

Friday night, Eden came over to hang out with Ruby and I. We didn't do much since none of us really were good at the whole girlie-sleepover thing, but we watched a few movies and talked about nothing of consequence. It was nice. Cole was there too, but he was working in his study. I tried not to think about the fact that he only stayed in case I lost control of myself, even if I wasn't expected to do that until the next night. I felt like I was counting down to the end of the world, and maybe it was at least as I knew it. Nothing would ever be the same after I changed into the banshee and made my first kill. Ruby had sort of tried to explain it, explain what it was like for her when she turned and couldn't control her bloodlust, but my case would be a lot different to hers. She made me feel like it was a responsibility of mine, rather than a misfortune like Sal had said, but I felt like it was a curse that I had been burdened with, a fate that gave God time off from being the 'bad guy' who kills good people – or beings. It still didn't sit right with me. I couldn't comprehend the logic. Maybe Sal was right. Some things couldn't be explained, they didn't have answers, they just were. I resented that sentiment.

On Saturday as night fell, after an early dinner, Cole, Ruby, and I headed to the cemetery to wait out for my change. Cole

198

reasoned that people already thought the cemetery was haunted, so it wasn't as much of a risk if I got seen after the change. I could only hope that I would be hanging around in the cemetery after changing, but I didn't like my chances. From what I saw of banshees, they moved fast, and they stayed hidden, well mostly. A flicker of white was the only trace that I had encountered on my first exposure, and that was more than anyone else saw.

I hadn't wanted to go into the Amund tomb with Cole and Ruby, because it didn't feel right to be in there creating more memories. I wanted to remember it from the last time I was there when it was just Harper and I. So instead I just lingered by the doorway, staring out at the neighbouring headstone that seemed to be decaying.

"Cole, why couldn't the wendigo come on holy ground last time?" I asked. "What makes them different to all of the other supernaturals that can, which is like, all of the rest of them?"

Cole smiled weakly. "They're impure because they feed on the flesh of humans and they don't need to."

I gave a shiver. "So, um, they're pretty much just human cannibals? How does that make them supernatural?"

"Well, I suppose they're not *super* or *natural*," he mused. "But they are a threat, and they do possess certain qualities as a result of that. They're fast, their hearing is acute, their sight is beyond compare to regular human sight, and their sense of smell is second only to a werewolf's."

"So, it's just the human flesh diet that makes them that way?"

He shrugged. "I have never made an acquaintance with one to be sure, but... well, *consuming* humans, killing them and ingesting them... that has its own repercussions. The soul that it has stolen is not laid to rest. They snatch it from the person and keep it for themselves. I can only assume that it has an effect on the creature, also in giving them the qualities it does and transforming them into what they are."

I frowned at the thought – a stolen soul not laid to rest and kept by the heinous and grotesque monster. I had been hunted by a wendigo, and I had almost been caught by one. Perhaps my fate of a banshee was a little bit better than the alternative, even if I cheerfully would have chosen neither. Even now, with my soul apparently intact, I would have to deliver a death sentence to other supernatural beings and, what, *set their soul free?*

"Do banshees hunt wendigos?" I asked.

Cole shook his head. "I cannot answer for sure."

"How else do they die? Or do they just keep hunting and feeding on humans until someone like you or Harper stops them?"

"Perhaps, or hunters like Leo stop them," he answered. "Though they are not well favoured amongst the supernatural, for the fact that you pointed out – they're not really supernatural, but also because they hunt innocents."

"What do vampires do then?" I frowned. "Or werewolves? Why does Harper need to leave to protect me? Or *did,* I suppose."

Cole's silver eyes flashed to a pacing Ruby and back to me.

"Yes, vampires and werewolves can lose control and take advantage of those less equipped to defend themselves. But we all tend to take precautions to ensure that does not happen. Vampires can feed on donated blood and survive, werewolves can lock themselves away. Wendigos only survive for the sole reason that they abuse the balance of nature."

"Sorry," I sighed. "I didn't mean to offend you."

"You didn't, Taylor, I understand that you're curious," he answered.

I bit my lip and checked my watch. It was only just going eleven thirty.

"So, how do you kill a wendigo then?" I continued. "You and Harper killed it last time, didn't you?"

Cole pressed his lips together, and his drawn eyebrows cast a shadow over his glittering eyes. Ruby stopped her pacing and looked up, her expression was wary.

"What?" I sighed. "Don't you think that I can take it?"

"It's not exactly pleasant."

I looked to the side. "Well, in about half an hour, I'll be killing something myself. So if you could tell me, even just to make me feel better about scratching something, then that would be sort of brilliant."

Cole smiled sympathetically at Ruby and then looked back to me.

"Well, after we caught it—"

"You and Harper?"

"Yes, Harper and I." He nodded. "We—"

"Who actually caught it? You or Harper?" I interrupted

201

again. "Because I know that it hurt Hunter before it started chasing me, but the next thing *I* knew I was slamming into Harper and the thing was dead."

"I caught it; vampires are faster than werewolves in human form." He smiled. "Harper ripped its heart out."

I nearly choked. "What? It's heart? What?"

"The heart needed to be removed, the body burnt, the heart submerged in holy water."

"Holy water?"

"To release the trapped souls."

My eyebrow rose. "Vampires have that sort of stuff lying around then?"

"It never hurts." Cole smiled. "After that, the heart is buried in holy ground."

"Why? Why give the monster that sort of respect?"

Cole tipped his head. "Everything that was living deserves respect."

I pressed my lips together. "Well, I'm clearly going to make a lousy banshee."

"I'm sure you'll do a fine job, Taylor," Cole answered. "Not everything is as atrocious as a wendigo. If banshees do not deal with them, then that's all the better for you."

"So, I just have to kill the decent supernatural beings then?" I muttered. "Awesome."

"We all have our shortcomings," Ruby replied. "Unfortunately, despite our best efforts, innocents have still died because of our existence."

Cole moved his arm around her, and she turned into him.

The two seemed to share a memory between them. Sal had said once that Ruby had killed a few men, and I didn't know the details, but knowing Ruby now, I couldn't see how she would have done it in *cold blood*. She was kind and fiercely justice-driven. Whatever it was, it didn't make her any less my friend or any less the person inside that vampiric circumstance.

I looked away and stepped outside the tomb into the pathway, beginning to pace myself. I wasn't embarrassed by the display of affection, but I was craving it for myself. I missed Harper, and I was terrified of what was to come. I hoped that he had gone far enough that I wouldn't see him before the Full Moon turns waning.

"Are you okay, Taylor?" Ruby asked, her voice a little muffled by Cole's shoulder.

I looked up and nodded. "I'm fine, I'm just… you two don't have to worry about watching me. I'm just going to drown in my thoughts, and try and get some fresh air to clear my head. I should be human until midnight, at least."

"Do you to talk about it? It might help?"

I smiled. "Thanks, but it won't. I just miss Harper, and it's all hard enough going through this without knowing that he's going to be hurting tonight with his change too."

"Of course."

"So, you can play chess or something. I'm just going to think to myself for a bit."

The vampires laughed.

"If you'd prefer it, we can leave you to your thoughts," Cole answered. "But we'll be right here if you need us."

"Thanks," I breathed. "With your hearing, I'm sure you'll be out in a flash if anything happens."

Ruby nodded and smiled.

I sighed and dug my hands into my jean pockets, stepping toe to heel up and down the uneven concrete slabs in the entrance of the tomb. Being back here with them and not with Harper just reminded me of when I had been here for my protection from the world, and it seemed strange to me that now I was here because it was the world that needed protecting from me. Similarly to last time though, I felt as if I was being watched like some kind of hopeless child that couldn't look after herself. I knew that it wasn't how it was now, but I still couldn't help but feel it. Unlike last time though, my supernatural support didn't have knowledge of what I was facing. This time they were as blind as me. In fact, the only person who knew anything about what to expect was...

"Sal," I sighed. "Hi."

"Taylor Mistry," he said. "By moonlight... at midnight. It's a midnight Mistry."

"You're so cheesy," I groaned. "And it's not midnight yet."

His head tipped. "Of course."

"What are you doing here? Is this your mothership or something?"

"Mothership? The cemetery? Nuh, all the clients are already dead. I'm here for you."

"Me? Why? Am I dying?"

He rolled his eyes. "You're not my area, remember? No, I knew that you were worried about changing, and considering for obvious reasons Wolfie can't be here…"

"Sal—"

"Sorry, *Harper*," he amended.

I sighed. "You didn't need to come. I have vampire back-up."

"All the more reason." He shrugged.

"They're not as bad as you make them out to be."

"Not actually what I meant," he replied. "I mean, sure they know what it's like to die and kill someone, but they don't know what it's like to experience death and *live* through it."

I looked up as the moonlight caught the glint of pale skin as Cole looked out from the tomb. When he saw that I wasn't alone, he stepped back inside along with his dull, supernatural glow.

I turned back to Sal. "Can I ask you something?"

"Do you think that I'd say no?"

I rolled my eyes. "What is with the illumination thing?"

"Illumination?"

"The glowing," I murmured. "They shine – the supernatural sort of gleam like they're incandescent to different degrees. It started last night after midnight, I guess."

He smiled ruefully. "What do you think it means?"

"I think that it's probably a banshee thing." I shrugged. "Since no one else noticed that my boyfriend started flickering with light."

He frowned. "Flickering?"

I nodded. "What does that mean?"

"I've never heard of that before."

205

"Did Alba tell you about seeing the glowing?" I asked. "Did you know about it?"

"She mentioned something about reading life energies," he replied. "She never expanded on it, so I figured it was sort of like what I see, but in humans, it's a sort of shadow or darkness, not a light. I guess being *super*natural, you get the glitter and glam."

I looked towards the tomb. "But the vampires are dim."

"Probably because they're undead and immortal." He shrugged. "Like I said, humans go dark, vampires aren't really dead, they're sort of in-between, like purgatory, but on earth."

I bit my lip. "So, the brighter the light…?"

"I guess we'll find out soon enough."

"What does the supernatural look like to you if humans are shadowy?"

"Nothing, there's just nothing," he said, looking at me a little more intently. "I guess there's a little fringing glow around the edges."

"Is that what you see in Harper too? Do you see the flicker? What would a flicker mean then?" I frowned. "Like, half-dead? Or…"

"Soon to be?" he offered. "I honestly don't know, Taylor."

I shook my head, glancing up at the Full Moon. "I can't do this."

"You don't really have a choice."

"What if I did?" I murmured. "Harper managed to not kill me last time. Maybe I could use the same resistance."

Sal's face wrinkled. "Reaping really doesn't work that way.

We don't decide on who lives and who dies, we just help with the transition."

"So what does decide? Fate?"

"Fate," he sighed. "God, a spirit in the sky, whatever you believe in."

I swallowed. "What do you believe?"

"I believe that everything ends."

"That's morbid."

He shrugged. "Not really, makes you live in the present more."

"Maybe," I mumbled, feeling a sudden rush of cold to my head. I blinked it off and looked back to Sal. "In case you were interested, your light isn't as bright as some that I've seen. It's between a vampire and a shifter."

Sal's eyebrows lifted. "Well, I guess there's your answer, I—"

His voice cut off as I doubled over, clutching my head. I peeked up at him and saw that he was frowning too.

"I need to go," he sighed. "Are you okay?"

My teeth were clenched as I nodded. "Is it, ugh, is it Jesse, *ow.*"

"You know that I can't—"

I reached forward and clutched his forearm, locking the grip.

"Taylor, you can't come," he whispered. "You're changing, it's too danger—ouch!"

Another roll of pain shot through me, from the crown of my head to the ends of my fingers, and the tips of my toes. It hurt, but it was almost a good hurt because what I felt after it was strength.

Sal pried my hands from his arm, and I exhaled, looking up as he closed his eyes. Using my new surge of strength, I reached out to grab his elbow as he sucked himself away.

I gasped as I felt myself being pulled, saw a flicker of my unit and heard Jesse's wail before I felt myself being twisted back to the cemetery. I flew back, ricocheting off a crumbling headstone like I was propelled from the eye of a sonic boom.

"Taylor!" Ruby exclaimed. I looked over at her and heard her sharp intake of breath as she saw my face. Cole appeared beside her in a flash and pushed her behind him. I put my hands to the ground to push myself up to stand and found myself standing in the next second.

"Ruby, get inside," Cole said quietly.

"No, I won't—"

His head tipped toward her. "Go."

I couldn't understand what they saw or what these immortal blonde vampires were scared of. As I lifted my hand to stop my friend from fleeing from me, I was momentarily distracted by the glint of my white skin in the midnight moonlight. It was so white that it looked almost transparent, and my nails – my nails were shining silver, and the ends of my hair were as blonde as Jesse's, platinum even, white. I opened my mouth to speak, but the only thing that came out was a scream that made Cole grab a frozen Ruby and dart away.

I couldn't understand it, but then I felt it. I felt all of them, and I felt myself being drawn away. It was an almost overwhelming urge to be elsewhere.

I turned and started to run, each stride covering kilometres, like a silver bullet shot through a cloud. I could feel the life forces as if they were glowing little candle lights amidst the human shadows, and I knew with every silver cell of mine where I needed to go. I breathed them in, I felt their pulse, I followed the lights, and there were a lot of them. The brighter they were, the more intense my compulsion to extinguish the flame, and one was brighter than the rest of them, so like a moth, gravitated towards my target. Distance didn't matter.

I was there in moments that felt like seconds, and the scream bubbled in my throat as my object neared and my other senses seemed to seep back into consciousness.

I arrived in a clearing that must have been on the north side of Half Moon Bay, on the fringe of shrubbery and woods. I hadn't been here before, but it didn't matter. I didn't plan on staying long.

My light-tinted vision began to clear, and amidst the glowing, I saw faces, two faces and the bloodcurdling scream forced its way out of my throat. I saw them both cringe as my own hearing began to clear, and then I heard his accent speak to me.

"Please, no," his beautiful French accent said. It wasn't exactly the one that I had fallen in love with. I turned towards André and let out another scream, watching cautiously as he shifted down into large paws and brown fur.

"Hey, banshee," the Spanish voice snarled. It was Hunter. Hunter, who had once tried to save me, though now she was

209

ready to attack me. "Stay back! Stay away from him!"

I could smell her fear, I could taste the tension rolling down her trembling arms, and I longed to reach out and touch them, to bring death upon her as if it was my mission. She wasn't who I came for, but she'd do, I would take her. I took a step towards her.

"Stay back!" Hunter repeated, jabbing something silver at me that she was gripping with a rag. It made me pause as I noticed it – the very silver dagger that I had removed from Harper, the blade that I had plunged into the last screaming woman in white that I had come across. It was the dagger that made me this way. It made me pause, but it didn't stop me. I couldn't stop, I needed to end the *supernatural* life and scream their swan song. I was conscious of Taylor, but I wasn't in complete control of her. I *was* in *complete* control of the banshee though, and she was telling me that it was the *rightest* thing to do. I needed it. The urge to take that life was outstanding.

The large predatory animal roared, and I swiped my nails in his direction, feeling the fur brush the tips of my fingers, but otherwise not making contact. He scampered back and gave another snarl as Hunter took another jab at me with the dagger, glazing the silver along my arm. I felt it burn as it tore the skin open, but it otherwise didn't bleed. Apparently, the dagger didn't have a lasting effect if it didn't stay entrenched in my flesh. Regardless, I screamed again, taking another slash at Hunter, sensing her light becoming as bright as her companion's. There was another roar from behind me, from the cougar, as André snapped at my leg; his teeth barely grazed

210

my near-impenetrable skin. He was close, so I lifted my hand, sweeping my knuckles across his tan-coloured muzzle, which sent him flying backwards into a thick tree trunk. Hunter made a strangled sound of protest as a sharp stabbing shot up my side from the silver dagger that plunged below my ribcage. Her hands were shaking wildly, but I could see that she was trying very hard to remain in human form as to not give me the advantage of opposable thumbs. I grabbed her by the throat and crushed her up against a nearby tree as André's roar to my left was drowned out by another almighty growl in the clearing. This growl didn't belong to a panther, it belonged to a wolf, and it made my joints lock in place.

No, not Harper, no. I felt his energy, his life, and with each flicker, I felt him draw me close and repel me, light on, light off, slay, revive, supernatural, super*normal*? I couldn't understand it – was it because he was half human-half wolf, or because he'd been almost marked and lived to tell the tale? What did that mean for him now? What did that mean for us?

I didn't want to go up against Harper, and even as a banshee, I could feel it in my heart that I didn't want to kill him. Harper wouldn't survive another banshee attack, and I didn't know myself enough to control the urge to kill if he attacked me. *If he attacked me.* Did he want to attack me? I was about to find out.

My grip on Hunter tightened as I turned just in time to see Harper launch himself towards us, leaping to attack, not me, but Hunter. I jumped back as he landed on her torso and snarled a slobbery bark in her shocked face.

"Harper! What are you doing?" she cried. I'd never seen her look so devastated. Even in my attack-mode, I registered that for a second, but it could only be a second because Hunter was fighting back, throwing Harper off her and into another tree. I twisted, feeling the dagger pulse in my side and pulled it out at the same time André leapt at me.

I dropped the dagger, reaching my fingertips towards him as his fangs snapped at me, his roaring cry echoing off the wood of the trees.

"No!" Hunter shouted, tearing herself from Harper's claws and stumbling over towards the whining and dying cougar. "André, André, no!"

She seemed to mourn only for a moment, before snapping into a rage. Her quick dark eyes moved towards the dagger as her faster hands reached for it. She rose, lifting it towards me as I felt the strength in my muscles weaken. The white glow of my hair and skin dimmed under the moonlight. I was becoming human again, I was becoming Taylor.

"Hunter," I said – said, not screamed because my words were back, I was human. "Don't, I'm sorry, I—"

Hunter growled, throwing the outstretched dagger at me as I cringed inward to anticipate the kill-shot into my chest... but it didn't come. Death didn't come. Harper did.

I heard his whimper as a loud thud sounded on the ground. I saw his fallen wolf-form harbouring the silver dagger as I felt myself being pulled away from the clearing. It was the strangest thing, not unlike the feeling that I had when travelling with Sal to his reaping, but different in the sense that it was like moving

212

through a vortex. Everything moved so quickly around me, until I found myself back in the cemetery, slamming up against the same headstone that I'd hit after being pushed by Sal's shockwave.

"Taylor Mistry," Sal sighed.

"Harper," I panted.

"It's Sal," he answered. "Salvatore Vincent, remember?"

I shook my head. "No, Harper's hurt, I need to go to him I… Sal."

His eyebrows lifted.

"You left, you… you went to my unit to reap someone as I was changing," I said. "Who was it?"

His expression darkened, which was something considering it was pitch black with all but the Full moonlight to shed any kind of light.

"Taylor, I'm sorry—"

"What did you do?" I screamed. "Who did you take?"

"I don't get to choose—"

"What did you do?"

Sal clenched his jaw. "You should get to Iris Memorial."

I shook my head. "No! Not until you tell me *who* you took."

"That's not for me to tell."

My fists slammed hard on his chest, and he flinched but straightened. "Taylor, go, your family needs you."

I let out a cry and shook my head. "No, I can't. I can't."

His arm reached around to support my back, and I pushed him away. "No."

My phone rang, and I looked around and found it in the

dirt with a blocked number lighting up on my screen. I could barely make it out through the blur of tears that were tumbling down my face.

"No."

"I'll drive you," he murmured.

I tried to control my hysterical breathing. Every inhalation tore at my throat like the air was made of razor blades.

"What about Harper?"

"Would you prefer to go to him?"

I swallowed, it hurt. "I don't know where he is for sure. I don't know if he's still alive."

Sal waited, his eyes speaking the words that he wasn't prepared to say. I needed to choose, Harper or my family—my blood, my twin—even if there was nothing that I could do for either of them. I let out a ragged breath.

"Take me to the hospital."

Phase Eight
The Aftershock

I talked myself in and out of a lot of things on the way to Iris Cove Memorial Hospital. I tried to tell myself that Harper was all right, that he would heal from the dagger, another dagger attack, and that he would be okay. I tried to tell myself that Hunter wouldn't react and want to kill me for what I did to André, and that she would understand that it was something that I didn't have complete control over. I tried to tell myself that I wasn't going to the hospital to find Jesse in the morgue, that maybe Brandon was right about his brain tumour and it was him that I was going to see. I didn't wish his death, but I just couldn't fathom not hearing Jesse's laugh again, or feeling his heartbeat that seemed to beat in time with mine. My twin, my best friend. It couldn't be him.

I tried to channel him, to feel him like I used to be able to, and maybe it was the Full Moon or the fact that my mind was obstructed with flashes of Harper being stabbed, but I couldn't, I couldn't, I...

"Tell me that it's not Jesse." I sobbed. "Sal, you have to tell me that you didn't take Jesse."

"Taylor."

"I can't. I can't feel if he's alive, I think used to be able to feel if he was okay, and I can't."

He glanced at me with his orange eyes but didn't reply.

"Sal, so help me, if you don't tell me, I will kill you," I growled. "Next Full Moon I will find you, and I will—"

"You can't kill me, Taylor."

I blinked. "Yes I can, you're supernatural, and I'm a supernatural reaper—"

"I am also death," he replied. "You only get to kill death once."

"What? What does that mean?"

"What I said."

I scowled at him, annoyed that he had distracted me from my rage, but the curiosity burnt deeper. Sal looked over at me and sighed.

"You killed a banshee to become one," he explained. "I told you that the reaper who took my family had mercy on me, but perhaps a better term was that I had mercy on him, so we made a trade: his death for my life. To become a reaper, I had to kill the previous one. That's the only thing that will set us free."

I stared at him in horror. *Set us free?* Death was the only thing to set us free?

"I'm not cynical of life, I enjoy being alive, but I know to stay this way, I need to work for it, and I need to defend for it," he added. "I see a lot of death in my life and you will too, Taylor. We can't control fate as much as we will it; some things

216

just need to happen to keep the balance."

I tried to understand what he was saying, but it all felt like too much to think about in light of everything else that had happened tonight.

"Are you telling me that the only way I'll die is if someone kills me?" I murmured. "That every Full Moon until that happens I'll need to kill someone else?"

"At least it's only once a month for you."

"But you don't *choose* who dies, right? You just attend their deathbed."

Sal's annoying black eyebrows rose. "Did it feel like a choice to you?"

"That's not the point. The point is that killing someone and easing someone's suffering are two *very* different things. One is murder, one is euthanasia."

"The ethics board might not agree with you on that one."

I clenched my teeth, and threw my back into the seat as we pulled in front of the brightly lit complex where Jesse worked... works? Worked? I blinked back tears that I wasn't sure were fuelled by anger or sadness.

Sal had barely stopped the car when I flung the door open and darted out, stumbling over my own feet a bit before I found them and ran through the doors of the emergency department.

"Can I help you?" a frowning clerk asked.

"I'm Taylor Mistry—"

"You're Jesse's sister, or Jack's daughter."

I exhaled. "Both, I guess, I... is... is Jesse here? Or my

217

dad… or Mum… or…"

She frowned again. "Right this way, Taylor."

Not a good sign when the emergency clerk personally escorted you in. She led me through the emergency department, past all the white curtains, and the island that was the nurses and doctor's station in the middle. I had been through here before, so the size and whiteness didn't surprise me, nor did all the little rooms that broke off for observation and holding bays.

The frowning clerk slowed by the family grief support room, and I recognised Brandon's tuft of blond hair standing outside it. He was leaning up against the wall with his head down and his hand shielding his eyes.

My heart sank. Not Brandon, but enough to upset Brandon. My knees locked in place and the clerk frowned back at me. Brandon looked up.

"Taylor," he sighed. "Why are you covered in blood?"

I blinked at him; not understanding his words then looked down. *Blood?* Oh, my arm. The cut from the silver dagger that Hunter had sliced me with was now a gaping wound, and my side was also red and seeping. I hadn't really noticed it when I was a banshee, but I guessed that human Taylor was a little less durable, and the hunter's dagger was the only thing that could really leave a mark.

"I'm fine," I murmured as the frowning clerk waved a doctor over. I side-stepped the lab coat and fixed my eyes on Brandon. "Where's Jesse?"

His lips puckered. "Taylor."

218

"Where is he, Brandon?"

The door beside him opened and another blond head peered out. Dad or Jesse? Why did they look so similar?

"Tay?" his broken voice cracked further.

I felt tangible relief surge through me that made me a little lightheaded. "Jesse."

He hastened towards me, nudging the doctor that was trying to assess the cut on my arm out the way, and pulled me hard against him.

"I'm so glad that you're here," he breathed. "I tried calling, but you didn't answer. How did you know?"

"I just did."

He pulled back to look at me and nodded, *we just did.*

"Why are you bleeding?"

I shook my head. It so wasn't important right now. "I... a tree scratched me."

His head dropped to my side, and he lifted my shirt to reveal the stab wound. It didn't look as gnarly as I thought it would, given the size of the dagger. Maybe I had managed to heal a bit since pulling the silver out.

"A tree did this?" He frowned, his voice flat. "Was it holding a knife?"

"Jesse, why are you here?" I exhaled.

Pain – extreme agony flickered in his light grey eyes that squeezed my heart in an excruciating, almost crippling manner.

"Ashley."

My breath caught in my throat. "Ashley?"

Jesse started crying, and my chest felt like someone had

replaced my heart with a grenade that had just erupted. Jesse never cried.

Brandon stood up and walked over, taking Jesse's arm as he folded to stop him from collapsing in a heap. I reached out for my brother's face and sank to my knees, feeling for the first time the pinch in my side.

"What happened? Tell me what happened," I whispered.

Jesse was in no state to talk, so it was Brandon who responded to my question.

"Her phone charger."

"What?" I snapped. His answer maddened me for some reason. "What do you mean?"

"It electrocuted her," he sighed. "The damn thing electrocuted her."

I wanted to throw up. Jesse always told her that her charger looked risky. *You should use my charger, darling. The one you're using looks dodgy. I don't even think it's a proper one.*

"How does that even happen?" I breathed, lifting to stand.

"Circuitry? Or maybe the electricity in the unit isn't properly grounded?" Brandon shrugged as Jesse stumbled back into the grief-room.

"But it's a phone charger." I said. "A *phone charger*."

"I don't know, Taylor!" Brandon exclaimed. "But it killed her. She's dead."

I felt hollow inside. Ashley and I were closer than we had ever been in recent times. We finally understood each other, and I actually had begun to like her, even think of her as a sister or a sister-to-be. But that was nothing compared to the love that Jesse felt for her, *nothing*. If even for him, my heart was shattered. She was too young. She was too alive to die.

I heard Brandon groan and looked up to see him clutch his head, then keel over himself, falling to the polished white flooring.

"Help!" I shouted, sinking to the ground as Brandon sucked shallow breaths through his teeth. His face went red and began to burn up. "Somebody!"

The medical emergency team seemed to be right behind me, pushing me back as they came to his aid. *Not Brandon, Jesse can't lose Ashley and Brandon.*

I sat back on the floor watching the navy blue and white-clothed bodies cluster around. My side began to throb harder now that I was crouched over, so I pressed my fingers into it, feeling a pulse of wetness under the tips.

"Hey… hey, are you all right there?" a faraway voice asked. I felt my shoulder being moved and blinked up at the blue-scrubs and bright ceiling.

Follow the lights. My eyes sank closed.

*

I woke to beeping. I hated beeping, the annoying high-pitched screech of artificial machinery that had no indication of feeling, just of vitality. I may be alive, but it was annoying me to death.

"Hey," a voice murmured, and I felt a hand on mine. "Taylor Mistry."

221

My eyes opened. "Salvatore Vincent."

"Relax. You're not dead, or dying."

I groaned. "Wonderful. Where's Jesse?"

"With the blond guy."

"Brandon." I blinked. "Where is he? Is he alive?"

Sal's orange eyes lifted and my head turned to the bed beside mine. The beeping wasn't coming from me. I wasn't even attached to anything. It was connected to Brandon. Brandon was alive, Jesse was asleep between us.

I tried to sit up, and my back was stiff, but I otherwise didn't hurt. My hand ran over my bandaged arm, and I pulled off the gauze to find a faint pink line.

"Um, keep that on there, Mistry," Sal whispered, pressing it back in place. "Docs don't like things they can't explain."

I exhaled and sat back. "Everything sucks."

"You're alive, your brother's alive," he noted. "Not everything."

I nodded and looked over at Jesse, my heart lurching for him. His sun-kissed skin was splotchy and red; his face looked worn, older somehow. He'd gone through too much tonight. He was only human.

"Ashley," I murmured. "You took Ashley."

Sal frowned. "It was her time."

"She was electrocuted."

"It was bound to be something."

I felt my forehead pinch. "Did you know that it was coming? Is that the *nothing* you saw when Jesse was hospitalised?"

He didn't reply, but I could see the affirmation in his eyes. *It was bound to be something.*

"I need to call Harper," I sighed. "I need to make sure that he's okay."

"Then I'm guessing it wasn't him?"

"What wasn't him?"

"Your hunt?"

I shook my head.

"Who was it?"

I shrugged. "André… or Hunter. I don't know, either would have done. But it was André."

"Shifters?"

"Panthers – a cougar and a jaguar," I mumbled. "Hunter is going to kill me when she finds me."

"She can try."

Jesse stirred and I paused to make sure that he wasn't going to wake up. His droopy head slumped deeper into the chair.

"She has a dagger, a silver hunter's dagger," I breathed. "The one that, well, fated me to this."

Sal glanced at my arm. "Oh, crap."

"What would happen if she used it on me? Would she become—?"

"No, she's already something else."

I took another glance around me. "So, I would just cease to exist?"

"I honestly don't know, Taylor. I've never known someone in your circumstance. Normally banshees don't make acquaintances with their prey, so they don't know them to hunt

223

them."

I rubbed my head.

"What happened to the... to Harper?" Sal asked. "If not you?"

"He tried to defend me and got stabbed himself," I whispered. "I changed back and got sucked away just as he fell."

Sal's eyebrows lifted, shedding light in his sunrise-coloured eyes. "He defended *you*? Like, he turned on his friends for you?"

"His oldest friend."

"Well, that is highly unusual." He frowned. "He should have a natural, survival instinct, flight response around a white woman."

"I told you that we're different. He loves me."

"He defies science. You both sort of do in being a couple."

I smiled humourlessly. "Science isn't always reliable. Some things you can't explain."

Sal chuckled. "Touché."

I looked back at Jesse. "Did you see my brother when you went to get Ashley? I thought I heard him scream out, was he hurting when I changed?"

"I didn't take a lot of notice, but I think the scream was more emotional pain than anything else." He pouted. "Maybe because you've transitioned your *other* side doesn't affect his human side."

"How do you mean?"

"Well, when you were changing over those three Full

Moons, you were still part human as well as supernatural." He shrugged. "Your two selves were mashed together, but now they're separate. You're only one now, so maybe he won't be affected by you at all."

"Because I'm not human any more?"

He mashed his lips together. "Well, yes, but that's a good thing if he was only linked to human you."

"That's very scientific, Sal."

"I told you that I passed high school science." He smirked and then cringed. "I have to go, Taylor Mistry."

I nodded. "Thanks for being here."

"Anytime," he said, standing and resting a hand on my shoulder. It fell away, and he exhaled, glancing over at the sleeping boys before popping away into nothing.

I drew in a deep breath and let it out, then jumped as someone with red hair appeared by my side. I half expected it to be Eden, but it wasn't. It was Ruby sporting her red wig.

"Hi." She smiled weakly. "Are you okay?"

"What are you doing here?" I whispered. "You're still supposed to be in hiding."

"Sal called, I'm sorry we left you before. I never wanted—"

"Please, I would have if I were you. I'm glad that you're both safe."

Ruby smiled and then bit her lip. "So how did—?"

"It was terrible," I breathed. "It was André."

"André?"

I nodded. "Hunter fought back and attacked me with the silver dagger, but she got Harper instead. I don't know if he's

225

okay."

Ruby was frowning as she lifted her phone to her ear.

Phone, Ashley. Poor Ashley.

Ruby spoke too fast and quiet for me to comprehend, and then she slid the phone back in her pocket.

"Cole is going to them. He'll be in touch as soon as he knows anything."

I exhaled. "Thank you."

She rested her hand on my arm, and I felt her flinch, but she didn't move it.

"What's wrong?" I frowned.

"It tingles a little," she whispered. "I'm sure it's nothing."

"Or its silver. Sal said that I wasn't human any more. He said that I had transitioned fully. So what if that means that there is more silver in me?" I murmured. "Ruby, I don't know who I am any more... or what I am... or what any of it means."

"It will be fine," she answered. I admired her for speaking with such conviction when she was surely freaking out more than I was. I could see it in her silver eyes as she moved her hand to grip mine. "We will get through this together. All of us."

"But what if it's not safe that we're all together?"

Jesse drew in a breath and Ruby looked up as he yawned.

"Taylor?" he mumbled.

"Hey, Jesse," I answered, trying to keep my voice light.

"Ashley?" Jesse blinked, then frowned as his eyes pooled with tears. "Wait, no."

I glanced at Ruby, her red wig looked similar to the way that Ashley's hair is… was.

"Um, Jesse this is Ruby," I said.

He looked up, and the moisture spilled over. He brushed it quickly away.

"Ruby? The elusive Ruby?" he replied.

Ruby gave my brother a dazzling smile. "One and the same. I've heard a lot about you, Jesse."

He nodded. "Likewise, sort of. Actually, Taylor hasn't told me anything except that you're her friend."

"I suppose that's all that matters about me."

Jesse rubbed his eyes. "I'm sure it's not."

"Jess, what happened to Brandon?" I asked. "Did they say why he collapsed?"

"Fatigue, dehydration, I don't know. As long as he is alive, that's all I can really handle right now. I need to make some calls and tell people about… what happened."

I sat forward. "That can wait, Jess, it's the middle of the night."

I felt Ruby's eyes on me but kept mine on my brother as he stumbled to his feet and dragged himself towards the door.

"It can't wait, Taylor. She's dead, she's not coming back, and her family need to know… they need to know," he said.

He didn't wait for an answer, and I let him go. If this was the way that he needed to grieve, then I wouldn't take it away from him. Besides, I did agree that her family should be told, even if it was nearing three in the morning. It had been a long night.

"Did someone else die?" Ruby whispered to me after he'd left.

I nodded. "Jesse's girlfriend Ashley was, um, electrocuted last night."

"What?" she gasped. "Oh gosh, it wasn't Eden who did it, was it?"

"No, a faulty charger, or maybe the electrical wiring in our unit."

"That's horrible."

I sighed. "Such is death."

*

Sunday was a strange day. When the sun came up, it seemed out of place in the sky. Jesse tried to take care of everything in the only way that he knew how – the surgeon, the doctor, science, logic, but none of it made sense. Sal was right, sometimes there were no answers, and some things had no explanation. Life, death, fate, maybe we couldn't control any of it. Maybe we couldn't even control who we were and who we became.

Brandon got discharged from hospital on Sunday afternoon and returned to our unit to recover. I didn't even mind that he was there because it felt like it was where he belonged anyway. It helped to have him around with Jesse out of sorts. It was hard for him to be back where it all happened. I half expected him to go back and stay with our parents for a while, but he didn't want to leave me or the memories that he had created in the short time that we had been living in our own little home.

Jesse went to Ashley's house on Sunday night, so it was just Brandon and I. We didn't do a lot of talking, and we both ended up getting an early night. I was just counting down the hours until Harper would return from his Full Moon cycle – if he would return. Cole hadn't managed to find him or Hunter, and neither was contactable via phone. I might have gone searching for them myself if I wasn't needed at home. Ruby stayed in the apartment to wait for word, and apparently, Eden was going to lend a hand with the search too. The only thing with her, though, was that Weavers could only teleport to places that they'd seen. So as far as tracing them both, she had to have somewhere in mind to go. I tried to describe it, but it felt like a dream to me, a trance that I wasn't really sure was real. But, of course, it was real. My imagination sucked.

Monday morning, I left Brandon with Jesse, planning their guys week to Half Moon Bay, which they would leave for after Ashley's funeral. The hospital had given Jesse grief leave, and Brandon thought that it would be a good idea for them to get away for a while. I agreed, even though I didn't know whether I was facing a similar loss with Harper. I couldn't even fathom him being dead. I couldn't imagine a world where he didn't exist.

I headed over to Cole and Ruby's apartment building early to wait and see if Harper and Hunter would return there, as they had initially planned.

"How is everything at home with Jesse and Brandon?" Ruby asked. "Are they coping?"

"Brandon is fine." I shrugged. "Jesse is hurting quite badly though."

"I can understand that. It's never easy letting go of someone, especially when it is well before their time."

"Not according to Sal," I murmured. "He saw that her time was coming a while ago."

Ruby looked down. "Well, it's never easy losing someone that you love."

"What's going to happen, Ruby? What if Harper doesn't come back?"

"He will."

"Okay, and what then?" I frowned. "What if I'm poison to him, and it hurts him to be close to me? It's a fate worse than death to live without being with the person that you love."

She shook her head. "No, it's worse than death for them to die at your hand. But, sometimes, letting go before that happens is the best and hardest decision that you can make for someone you love."

I dropped my gaze to my hands and pouted. Harper and I had tried to be apart before. He'd left because he thought that if he stayed, my life would be in constant peril. But really, it was only when I was without him—when we were without each other—that neither of us felt safe or whole. Maybe I could survive without him, but it didn't feel much like living.

There was a rattle at the door, and I felt my heart rise to my throat.

Ruby sighed. "I told you he would be back."

I nearly fell off the stool as I clambered towards the front door and Harper half-staggered in holding his side. He looked up and smiled when he saw me, his expression looked weary, but beautiful, as always. I hastened forward and stopped half a step in front of him. I was too afraid to touch him just in case my skin had the same *tingling* effect on him as it had on Ruby.

Harper didn't have the same reservation though, and he stepped into me, scooping me up with his lips. If it hurt him to do so, he didn't show it. He pulled me close and breathed me in, moving his arms around me so I could feel his beating heart against mine. It was beating fast, he was alive, and we were on fire.

"I was so afraid," I breathed between kisses. "I was so scared that you were hurt, or worse, or—"

I was silenced by his lips, and there was nothing but the pulse of blood in my ears, the low moan in his throat, and the slight whimper in mine.

Harper pulled back. "What is wrong?"

"I love you."

He smiled. "How is that wrong?"

I pouted, and Harper looked behind me.

"Hello, Ruby." He nodded. "Apologies for my manners."

Ruby shook her head. "Not at all, Harper, I would have been offended if you didn't react as such."

Harper breathed a small laugh. "Is Cole not here?"

"He's at *Freeze Frame*, he'll be back shortly," she answered. "We were all worried about your condition after what Taylor told us. We tried to look for you but had no luck. Where is Hunter?"

231

Harper's brow furrowed. "Hunter left."

"What?" I sighed. "Why? Where? Where did she go?"

"Back to Spain to stay with her old friend. He's a vampire named Miguel," Harper explained. "I believe you know him too, Ruby."

"Yes." She nodded. "He and Cole are also old friends."

I shook my head. "She left because of me."

"She left because of what happened," Harper answered. "Which wasn't your fault."

"But she thinks it was."

"She lost a friend. She is hurting. She needs someone to blame."

I sighed. "And why not blame the person who killed him, right?"

"Taylor, stop. It was not your fault," he said. "You are merely a victim of circumstance. Every single one of us knows what it feels like to not be in control."

I frowned. "Maybe she's right to leave. Maybe you should all leave."

"No, I told you that I'm not—"

"You nearly died for me, again," I interrupted. "Again, Harper, you nearly died because of me. What happens when it's me that is driven to kill you? Do you really think that I'll be able to live with myself when the time comes?"

"*If*, Taylor," he answered. "And it's a big *if*."

I shook my head. "When."

"I'm not afraid."

"Really? Because I'm terrified."

232

He took my hands, and I felt them tremble between my fingers. It was only then that I realised that it did have some kind of effect on him to hold them with the silver pulsing in my body. Harper pressed his lips together and then looked up at Ruby.

"Can you please give Cole our regards, Ruby?"

She nodded. "Of course."

He looked back at me, and I glanced at Ruby and attempted a smile. I didn't know if I pulled it off, but she returned one that made me feel a little less afraid. Harper took my hand, leading me back down to my car. He drove us back to the little cottage that he called home in the interim that Hunter was away. I guessed that, since it was the case again, he would return to living there.

I told him about Ashley on the way, and about Brandon's hospital stay, and about how Jesse was coping. He didn't say much, but Harper never needed to. His eyes gave away everything that he was feeling, and it looked like he was feeling everything at once.

We walked through into the little lounge room and stood in silence, and then his arms encircled me again.

"We survived," he sighed.

"Barely," I mumbled, hugging him back tightly. "You got stabbed."

"I recovered."

I pulled back. "Did you?"

He lowered his eyes, and I lifted the bottom of his grey shirt up to his ribcage until I reached the raised, glowing pink scar that sat on his left side just below his heart. It didn't look like it had fully healed, which explained his slow movements. I wondered if it was the same as the last time that blade had pierced him.

"Is it because it was a silver hunter's dagger?" I asked.

"That, and because of its positioning."

I rested my hands on his chest. "Harper, Cole said that silver through your heart would have poisoned you. It would have killed you."

"Yes, but she didn't get my heart."

Hunter. Hunter didn't pierce his heart. His closest friend, his oldest friend didn't succeed in stabbing him through the heart while he was too busy trying to save me.

"This is all my fault," I sighed. "And now Hunter—"

He pushed his shirt back down. "It wasn't your fault, Taylor."

"But Hunter—"

"Is old enough to make her own decisions."

"Why aren't you mad at me?" I frowned.

"Why would I be mad?"

"For André. For Hunter."

"You had no control over either."

"You're right. I had *no control*. I have no control, which means you that might be my target come the next Full Moon." I shook my head. "I'll see your death coming and I can't... *I can't* be the one to do it, Harper. I can't."

"Taylor," Harper sighed. "I love you, and I know that you love me enough to resist killing me, just like I did with you."

234

"But what if love isn't enough?" I murmured.

"Love is always enough."

"You're so sure."

"I know who you are, Taylor, even if sometimes you are not so sure," he whispered, resting his hands on my arms.

"You might know who I am, but I don't. I don't trust myself enough not to hurt you, and I'm terrified that I will."

"You won't."

"You can't be sure of that. Sal said that I would have no control over it, and I *had* no control Saturday night."

"Do you think that every cell in my body didn't want to hurt you when you were marked?" he breathed. "Everything that I was told me it was the right thing to do, but I still managed to resist because my heart knew that it was wrong."

I frowned. "I'm not as strong as you, Harper."

"You're strong, Taylor, you are stronger than you know."

"Maybe you should be with someone who is better suited to you," I said. "Someone who understands you, who will protect you, and who won't pose as a threat to you or burn you with their touch."

His mouth fell open, and he looked down at his hands and turned them over. I could see a very slight redness in them. Not enough to bubble the skin but, I assumed, more like the feeling of the prickle of a battery on your tongue.

"Someone like who?" he asked. "I don't want anyone else."

"I don't want anyone else either, but I don't see any alternative. I'd rather see you alive with someone else than dead in my arms."

235

"There are more options than that. I won't give up on us."

I shook my head slowly.

"Taylor, you accept me as I am, in spite of all my shortcomings, so why won't let me do the same for you? Don't you think that you deserve it?" he asked.

"It's not about that, Harper," I sighed. "My flaws are fatal to you."

"I could have said the same to you once."

"You did."

His russet eyebrow rose. "And look how that turned out. Love means letting yourself be loved. Let me love you as you are, Taylor."

"I don't want to hurt you."

"That's for me to worry about."

"It won't be easy," I murmured. "Living like this won't be easy."

"Tell me what is easy?" he countered. "Certainly not life in general."

I bit my lip. "Apparently not death either."

"Well, if it's my fate to die, then there is no one else I would want to be by my side when it happens," he said, resting his forehead against mine.

I exhaled and lifted my fingers to brush his cheek and then blinked as the light surrounding him seemed to flicker in a fleeting glow. I stepped back.

"What?" he asked. "What is it?"

I shook my head. "The flicker, I… I thought that it would disappear when the Full Moon passed… or maybe because it's still close to the Moon phase that it's still there…"

His head tipped. "What flicker?"

"I can see a glow around supernatural people, beings, whatever," I muttered. "I didn't know what it meant until I changed into the banshee – the brighter the light is, the more at stake they are to be, well, hunted."

His frown deepened. "Mine is a flicker?"

I nodded. "It was more constant last Friday though, but now it's hardly there."

"What does that mean?"

"I don't know. Sal didn't know what it meant either. Normally they glow to varying degrees, or they're just dim, like the vampires. Yours is sort of dim until there's a flicker."

His eyebrows lifted. "Vampires don't glow?"

"Sal said it was because they were undead and immortal, so they're sort of in purgatory on earth."

"What about Weavers?" he asked. "Did you see what Eden's glow looked like?"

"What would Weavers have to do with it?"

"They're living immortals," he answered. "They heal with their blood, so the constant cell regeneration keeps them alive and young."

I frowned. "Do you think that because Rob gave you some blood a few months ago that it had an effect on you?"

His head rocked. "Perhaps, perhaps not. Werewolves operate in the same way, but we only heal when we're wounded, which is why we are not immortal, we age. Regeneration only occurs when prompted."

"So…" I said, biting my lip in thought. "So maybe because you've been healing a lot lately, your blood is in overdrive."

"Overdrive," he repeated. "So you think that I'm becoming immortal?"

"Stranger things have happened."

He smirked. "Not this strange. Werewolves are not immortal, I have never heard of any case to the exception."

"How much do you really know about werewolf lore? Have you met many others?"

"No one besides my father."

"What did he tell you?"

"The essentials, I suppose," he answered. "Cole might know more, he knew a werewolf many years ago. He has travelled more, seen more."

"Well, let's ask him." I nodded, taking a step back from him.

He caught my hand. "Not now, later. Now I just want to be with you."

I lifted my arms to encircle his neck, trying to bury my scientific curiosity. I wanted to know that he would be okay. I wanted an explanation for all the uncertainty. I wanted to know that the illogical could be logical.

"Taylor?"

"Hm?"

"You are distracted."

I shook my head. "Sorry, I just want to know that everything will work out."

"It will."

"How do you know?"

"Such is fate," he replied.

I sighed. "Such is death."

"Such is life," he whispered lowering his lips to mine.

Epilogue

Extra Ordinary

"Taylor Mistry," the guy behind the counter sighed as he took my paperwork. "Lost your identity, huh?"

I frowned. "Excuse me?"

"Your student identification." He smiled, pointing towards the payment slip. "Nothing personal."

"Oh."

"You don't remember me, do you?"

"Um, should I?"

"Ouch," he said. "We went out once a couple of months ago. I'm not really surprised that you don't remember. You seemed to be a little distracted at the time."

"Sorry, I guess I was." I nodded and stared at him. "Um, Theo, right?"

He smiled. "Right, I'm the surgeon."

"Surgeon? Then why are you—?"

"Computer surgeon." He chuckled, standing up and adjusting the camera. "Remember? You said you have a family of surgeons, and I said… never mind."

"I'm sorry, I… I'm a bit of a terrible person."

"For forgetting me?"

"For a lot of things."

"I'm sure that's not true," he replied. "Unless you're an axe murderer or something."

I tried to laugh, but it sounded off. *Nice try at nonchalance, Taylor.*

"Look here, Taylor," he said, pointing at a red spot. Above it was a yellow happy-face sticker. "Smile."

I worked to pull the corners of my lips up, and Theo pulled a face.

"You can do better than that, Mistry."

I exhaled and tried again. There was a flash that made me flinch.

"Easy," he sighed. "That was better. Do you want to check it before I print it?"

I shook my head. "Can't help what I look like, right?"

"You pull it off all right."

"So you work in student administration then?" I asked. "That's a bit lowly for a computer surgeon, isn't it?"

He chuckled. "I also help out in the library and information systems department to lend a hand with their technical issues."

"Well then, I take it back."

"It pays the bills. We can't all be superheroes."

"Who's a superhero?"

His head tipped as he glanced at the screen. "Don't you save helpless animals? That's pretty heroic."

"Maybe. It doesn't make me super though."

"If you say so." He smiled, handing me my new student

identification card. "Taylor Mistry, your new identity."

I glanced at it and sighed. "Looks like the old one."

"This one is more refined."

"How do you know?"

"The old one is on the system." He shrugged.

"Oh, wonderful," I groaned.

He chuckled.

"Well, thanks, I guess," I said. "And I'm sorry for not remembering you at first."

He reached out a hand towards me, and I took it.

"Taylor Mistry. He nodded.

"Theo…"

"Asimi," he replied. "Theo Asimi."

My brow creased. "Asimi?"

"Well, it's the English translation of my name. It's Greek, it means silver."

I laughed. "Silver, Greek, of course."

"I don't know why that's funny."

"It's not. South Coast is just pretty culturally diverse. There are a lot of Europeans here."

He shrugged. "I think there are more Brits, but whatever. Depends on what circles you hang out in, I suppose."

I nodded. "Thanks again."

"Maybe I'll see you around."

"Maybe." I shrugged. "If our circles collide."

He glanced to the side and smiled, it made me a little uneasy. "Somehow I think they will."

I turned slowly and found myself face-to-face with Harper.

"Oh, hi," I said.

"Are you identifiable?" he asked.

"Yes. I have a new identity, thanks to Theo."

Harper smiled weakly before his eyes glanced behind me. They seemed to harden as they settled on Theo.

"Come on," he whispered a little rigidly, taking my hand. "Let's go."

Before I could answer, he tugged on my arm, leading me out of the student administration office.

"What's wrong?" I muttered.

"Nothing."

I squeezed his hand and pulled back on his arm. "Harper."

He sighed. "The Greek."

"Theo? Why?"

He glanced at me warily, and I bit my lip.

"Because I went out with him once, after you told me to move on?" I asked. "You were watching me when I thought you had left that time, right?"

He frowned. "I didn't. No, that's not... that wasn't the reason, though it does concern me who you gravitate towards."

"What do you mean?"

"He's a hunter," he answered. "A wolf-hunter."

I blinked. "What? How? Why? How do you know?"

"The mark on his wrist. Didn't you recognise it? The Italian had one just like it."

The Italian, the Greek. Leo, Theo.

I had noticed that Leo had a tattoo on his wrist – a strange looking flower in dark purple ink. I hadn't thought anything of

243

it actually.

"I didn't notice anything on Theo." I shrugged. "But Leo said that his tattoo was a family symbol."

He nodded. "Family of hunters. Do you remember what it was?"

"A flower?"

"A purple flower. Wolfsbane."

"Wolfsbane?"

"It's poisonous to humans but fatal to werewolves," he murmured. "Hunters, specifically wolf-hunters, wear it as a mark of honour, a badge of what they stand for."

"Who stands for killing animals, and humans, and humans that shift into animals?" I asked, and then realised that banshees, in large part, did the same. "Well, who does that and are proud of it?"

Harper frowned and I hated the look of uneasiness on his face. I reached up to rest my hands on his cheeks.

"Taylor. Taylor Mistry," my name rang.

I looked up at the other Italian. "Sal. Salvatore Vincent."

"What are you doing here on winter term?"

"I failed a unit, so I had to make up the credit," I sighed. "Plus, I lost my identity."

Sal gave a short laugh. "Right, right. Hey, Wolf."

"Grim."

"He has a name," I snapped, and the two boys looked at me. "Harper, I mean."

Sal shrugged. "I have a name too. Sal—"

"We know," Harper and I answered in unison.

He grinned. "So are you coming or going?"

"Going," I answered. "To see vampires, so you wouldn't be interested in coming."

Sal pulled a face. "And I *really* wanted to be the meat of this masochistic sandwich. Darn."

I started to walk away and pulled Harper with me.

"Did you say that you lost your identity?" Sal asked, walking after us. "Do you mean your student identity?"

I groaned. "What else would I mean?"

He laughed. "So you met the Greek then?"

"I had met Theo before."

"I wasn't talking to you, Taylor Mistry," he answered. "I was talking to the wolf."

Harper stopped and pivoted, so he was staring Sal square in the eyes. Sal recoiled, then rocked forward to meet the challenge.

"What do you know of the hunter?" Harper asked.

Sal smirked. "I know that he didn't end up here by accident."

"Tell me that you didn't have something to do with him being here, Sal," I said through gritted teeth.

He huffed. "Please give me some credit, Taylor Mistry. I wasn't even a student here when he started here. I only discovered him when I enrolled, and he had to make up *my* identity card."

"How long have you—?"

"Irrelevant," Sal snapped, cutting me off. "Look, despite what you think, I don't hate your boyfriend. Besides, you have

245

been through enough the past, whatever, to have to deal with him being hunted down and killed by that Greek guy."

I cringed.

"So what are you saying?" Harper asked, his voice a little calmer than before, even though he was still eyeing Sal as if he didn't trust him as far, well, he could probably throw him further.

"I want to help." Sal shrugged.

I frowned. "Help what?"

"Help you get rid of this guy."

Harper's head tipped. "Who said that we're going to—?"

"Please," Sal sighed. "Give me *some* credit, you two."

"We're not going to kill him," I said. "No one is going to die under my watch."

Sal's eyebrow lifted. "You're a bit of a hypocrite, Mistry."

I pushed him in the chest with my hand. "Shut it, Salvatore. I don't have control over the… thing."

Sal's hand rested on mine on his chest. "I didn't mean killing him. Why would I want to kill anyone? Death is too much a part of my life as it is."

Harper nudged Sal back, so he was out of my reach, and my hand could fall away from him.

"Why do you want to help us?" Harper asked. "Not for me."

"No. Like I said, Taylor has been through enough." He shrugged. "What does it matter if you benefit from it, Wolf? Don't you trust me after everything that I've done for her? I've never lied to her, and I've even gone out of my way to help her."

"That's what I don't trust," Harper replied. "Your motives."

"My motives or Taylor?" he asked. "Because hey, there's nothing between us, but—"

I gasped as Harper stepped forward and in the same second had Sal by the collar of his shirt. Harper's skin seared against Sal's cross again, but Harper didn't flinch.

"Stop!" I shouted, more for Harper's benefit than Sal's. I stepped under Harper's arm and pushed him back. His grip loosened and he shook off his burnt hands.

"This is not helpful *at all*," I groaned. "Look, I... we don't even know if Theo will come after you, Harper—"

Sal's rolled his eyes as Harper's eyebrows lifted. The two of them made a similar sighing sound.

"Well, we don't." I shrugged. "We don't even know if he knows that you are... what you are, Harper."

"Oh, he knows," Sal muttered. "They always know."

I glared at him. "We have bigger things to worry about right now without—"

"I don't think that you quite understand what this means for him, Taylor," Sal interrupted again. One more interruption and I was going to scream. "Wolf-hunters may be human, but they're as thorough as banshees are when it comes to marking and killing their prey. If Theo has spotted Harper, he will pursue him. It's a part of their little mantra."

"Mantra?"

"You know a lot about this for a reaper, Grim," Harper

247

noted.

"It's South Coast, it's a beacon for supernatural things here," Sal answered. "You know as well as I do that hunters tend to hang around in places like this. It means that they have to travel less for work."

Harper didn't reply, and again, I hated seeing the worry on his face.

"What do you mean *bigger things to worry about*?" Sal frowned. "What could *possibly* be bigger than Wolfie's potential demise?"

I paused for a moment before replying. "His potential immortality."

"Come again?"

"The flicker, you know, the glow that he had that came and went?" I explained. "Well, it's all but disappeared now, it has only happened a couple of times since the last Full Moon since he had to heal himself again. We think that because he's had to heal himself so much that it's fundamentally affected his regeneration."

"Which is bad why?"

"It's not bad, it's just weird." I shrugged. "We want to know why."

Sal rolled his eyes. "Because you're scientists or sticklers for punishment? Why question something that's obviously a good thing?"

"Because we don't know enough about it to know if it is good," I snapped. "Sometimes it's good to ask questions and seek answers for things that you don't know much about."

"Have you thought about the fact that maybe you *can't* see

248

the illumination between the Full Moon? Maybe between changes you're just ordinary again?"

"What did you call her?" Harper asked.

Sal groaned. "I mean, gah, you know what I mean – normal, human-like…*non-banshee*."

"I get it," I sighed. "And I don't know, maybe I am. But I can still see the flicker when it happens. But I've got no one to test that theory on, because all of the other supernatural people that I tend to be around are immortal, undead, Harper, or, you know, you."

"Awesome?"

"Dead."

"Ouch," he mouthed. "So, how are you going to test it then, Mr and Mrs Scientist?"

I drew in a breath. "Cole ran some blood work. We are heading there to check out the results. Beyond that, I don't know."

Sal looked at Harper through narrowed eyes, and Harper's forehead creased. It cast a shadow over his pale, olive-green eyes.

"Nope, he's still not human," Sal answered. "So whatever he is, you can rule that out."

"Gee, thanks, we wouldn't have otherwise been able to deduce that," I muttered, looping my arm through Harper's and hauling him away.

"Are you going to the vampires now?" Sal asked.

"I told you, you're not coming."

"No, you said that you were seeing them and *assumed* that I wouldn't be interested in coming," Sal answered with a grin. "But as it turns out, I'm between semesters, and I've got some time on my hands."

"Don't you have someone to save or something," I groaned.

"Other than you? No." He shrugged. "Off-season, I guess. People die less out of semester when I *have* the time."

"I thought that you didn't want to be the third wheel?"

"I don't, but it's a fifth really, isn't it? Considering Doctor Vamp's blonde counterpart will probably be there too. I'm better at dealing in groups."

I exhaled. "You are insufferable."

"And you are rather cute when you're snippy, Mistry." He smiled. "Shall we?"

Harper gave Sal a murderous side-glance that only made Sal grin wider as we walked down to my four-wheel drive.

The drive was awkward, but luckily quick since Harper floored it around the tight South Coast streets. Sal hummed all the way, and I wanted to smother him with my sweater. It was a testament to my self-control that I didn't.

"Your blood work has changed slightly," Cole said, burying the unnecessary lead as he opened the door for Harper and me. His brow drew at Sal, but he stepped back to allow him in also.

"Changed?" Harper asked.

"How?" I echoed.

"Hey, Doctor Vamp, Blondie." Sal waved.

Ruby smiled politely at him, and Cole nodded.

"It's rather bizarre, but it seems to have taken on some

250

qualities similar to the Shadow Weaver's blood. Or kind of like a shifter, like Hunter's," he continued. "Taylor is right. The constant healing seems to be affecting you in a way that could result in slowing or ceasing your aging if it continues to evolve as it has. I fear that if you continue needing to recover, then you will freeze and remain in your current appearance indefinitely."

"You mean immortality?" Harper frowned.

"Yes. Something of the sort. Although it's not an exact science, I haven't seen anything like this before."

I bit my lip. It wasn't the worst news considering it looked as if I was going to be around until someone killed me and replaced me as a banshee. But I didn't plan on letting them get close enough again. Hunter's attack had been an eye opener, and I'd asked Harper to teach me some kind of combat just in case. It was probably redundant, but it was handy to know.

"Good news for you then, Mistry, banshees tend to stay away from immortals. Sounds like Wolfie is off your hit-list." Sal yawned, flopping on one of the chesterfields. "Nice place you've got here, Doc."

I looked at Harper and smiled weakly.

"Good news, it may be, but you are not out of the woods yet, Harper," Cole said. "You are currently still mortal. But as I said, there is a chance that may change."

Harper nodded. "I understand."

"Eternal youth is not something to take lightly – if that is a possibility for you. I suppose it is a choice that you need to make on whether forever is something that you want to face."

Harper's brow drew. "Forever... forever a slave to the Moon."

"Well, that decision can be put on ice for a while," Sal sighed. "If the Greek wolf-hunter has anything to say about it."

"Greek?" Ruby asked.

"Wolf-hunter?" Cole echoed.

Sal shrugged. "He works in admin."

"And the library apparently," I added.

"He saw you, Harper?" Cole frowned.

Harper nodded.

"Well, that certainly isn't ideal. Perhaps you don't have long to make your decision, Harper," Cole said. "We will protect you, of course, but one more serious wound could tip you over into immortality."

"Snuff the light," Sal sang.

"Shut up, Salvatore," I growled. "Your comments are not helpful."

He smiled. "They're not meant to be."

"Can I get you a drink or anything, Sal?" Ruby asked.

Sal stood up. "Sure, Blondie, what do you have that wasn't extracted from a human?"

The two went into the kitchen and Cole, Harper, and I clustered closer.

"Harper, as I said, this decision isn't one to make lightly," Cole murmured. "You will need to consider how it will affect you and Taylor. Being ageless means that you cannot stay in a place too long. Family may not be an issue, but any human contacts will need to be all but severed in due course."

I exhaled slowly. Was that the same for me too if I chose to stay with Harper forever?

"It won't be real immortality though, will it?" Harper asked. "I can still die, just not from old age."

"Yes, quite right. Silver will still affect you, as well as wolfsbane if you come into contact with the plant in any form."

Harper looked over at me then looked down. He pulled something out from under his shirt that was wrapped in a white cloth.

"What is that?" I whispered.

"The key to death," he said. "The answer to life."

I glanced at Cole who looked equally as curious as I was. Harper peeled back the cloth to reveal the silver dagger.

"I didn't trust leaving it in Hunter's possession when it is the only thing standing between your life, Taylor, and your death."

I looked at Cole then at Harper. "It can bring death upon any one of us."

"Or life," Harper murmured. "Eternal life."

"What are you saying?"

"This dagger will extinguish my light, eliminating me as someone that could die at your hand, Taylor. I want you to use it on me."

"No," I sighed. "I don't want to hurt you."

He exhaled. "Cole cannot touch silver without being burned."

"What if it doesn't work?"

"It will."

"But what if it doesn't only extinguish your light, it kills you?" I asked. "Cole, what if his blood doesn't regenerate him after another attack? What if you're wrong and it kills him?"

Cole's eyebrows lifted. "Given the mutation present that is representative of that of the Weaver's, I don't deem that likely."

"Not everything in medicine is reliable though." I frowned. "Everyone reacts differently to things."

"That is also true."

Harper offered me the blade. "It will work as long as it's not near my vitals."

I shook my head. "I'm not stabbing you, Harper."

"I'll heal."

"I'll do it," Sal said.

I shot him a glare, and he recoiled. My eyes found Harper's again.

"Please, Taylor," he breathed. "I trust you, only you."

I didn't want to do it, I didn't know if I could inflict pain on him on purpose, but I took the dagger from him and rolled it over in my hands. I could feel the energy from it, the magic embedded in it, almost as if it was sinking into my skin and flowing through my veins. Cole took a step back as Harper reached for my wrist and lifted it, so the tip of the dagger was to his side, just above his hipbone.

I shook my head. "Please, don't make me do this. I can't be the reason for you to be hurt again."

"I love you."

"Don't make me do it, Harper."

"I adore you."

254

"Please."

"To the Moon and back."

"No," I whispered as his grip tightened and he yanked my hand towards him. I gasped as he groaned in pain, his knees buckling as Cole fled around to catch his frame before it hit the ground.

"No, Harper," I cried out as Cole wrapped the blood spotted cloth around the handle of the dagger and withdrew it, laying it beside him. I removed my sweater and knelt beside him, pressing it to the gaping wound to stop him from losing too much blood before he had the chance to heal.

"Jesus, Mary, and Joseph," Sal muttered. "That was a bit dramatic."

"Shut *up,* Sal!" I screamed, my voice breaking with emotion. Ruby ushered him towards the couch as Cole's cold hands moved over mine to peel back the fabric to check Harper's wound.

"Is it healing? What's happening?" I sighed.

"Not yet," Cole answered.

Harper was panting, sucking air through his teeth as his body began to convulse.

"Cole, do something," I squeaked.

"I can't, it's just his blood reacting to the silver. It's like poison to him," he murmured.

I frowned.

"Plus, given the fact that he's in his human form, it's likely to take longer for him to heal," he added. "The paranormal abilities take longer to kick in."

I shook my head. "I shouldn't have let him do it, why did I let him do it?"

His silver eyes glanced up at me. "He made his own decision. It wasn't up to you to change his mind, Taylor."

I blinked back tears as the trembling stopped and he seemed to slip into unconsciousness.

"I'm going to move him to my study," Cole said. "He can recover in there. It'll also give you more privacy."

I nodded, and Cole shifted to pick Harper up. It was the first time that I could really appreciate how strong vampires were. To pick up a grown man from the floor who was not cooperating would have been a feat without him being laced with lean muscle.

Harper didn't wake until well after nightfall, and even though the seconds felt like minutes, the minutes felt like hours, and the hours felt like days, I didn't give up. By the time his pale green eyes fluttered open, I couldn't even bring myself to be angry with him for stretching my nerves to nothing as I waited.

"*Bonjour.*"

I sighed. "*Bonsoir.*"

"Is it night?"

"Yes."

"I'm sorry." He stretched, wincing a little. "I didn't think that it would take that long."

"You had me worried, but Cole assured me that you would heal in time."

He smiled weakly. "I always do."

I rested my head on his chest. "Don't do that to me again."

His hand reached up to stroke my hair. "Okay."

I could hear his heartbeat, and it somehow calmed me to know that now it would continue to beat for eternity, well unless...

"What are we going to do about Theo?" I asked.

"Nothing yet," he murmured, his voice sounding like a rumble under my ear. "But we will need to do something soon."

I looked up at him. "Do you think that we will need to leave South Coast?"

"Hopefully not. I know you have a lot of roots here."

"I would leave for you."

"I appreciate you saying that, but as I said, hopefully, it won't come to that. At least not in the foreseeable future."

I moved my arm around his abdomen and shuffled onto the couch beside him. Harper moved slowly to sit up a little, so I could fit beside him on the two-seater loveseat.

"Thank you," I whispered.

He looked down at me. "For what?"

"For what you did," I answered. "I don't like it, but I know why you did it. I'm not a threat to you any more, and you made that sacrifice for me even if it means that you will live eternally as a werewolf."

His arm around me tightened. "There are a lot of things that I would do for you, Taylor. That was nothing in comparison."

"I wish that I could do something for you."

"You already have," he murmured, his lips dropping to my ear. "You have given me a reason for eternal life."

I couldn't help but laugh.

"You laugh?" He huffed.

"Only because it's a little ironic that someone like me, who represents death, is the reason for your life," I replied.

"Ah." He chuckled huskily. "Such is death."

I smiled and twisted around to kiss him, feeling his body sink against mine as he kissed me back. We may not be the same two people as we were a few months ago—human and werewolf—but maybe that was okay, because we were better now, stronger both individually, and as a couple. We had overcome uncertainty, faced adversity, and death, and even when it didn't seem like there would be a light at the end of the tunnel, the sun broke out and set the sky on fire.

We were no longer in separate worlds, the ordinary and the extraordinary, we were in the same world now where Taylor and Harper, banshee and werewolf, could co-exist. It was by no means a perfect world, but we were perfect in it – perfectly imperfect, and completely out of control as supernatural creatures. Regardless, as far as I was concerned, forever with Harper may not be long enough.

But such is life.